KANTARA
THE TRAVELER

STEPHEN AND MARY WELLER

ISBN: 978-1-957723-99-0 hard cover
ISBN: 978-1-960146-00-7 soft cover

Edited by: Curt Locklear
Illustrations by: Tommy Guns
Cover design by: Sukesha Ray

Published by Warren Publishing
Charlotte, NC
www.warrenpublishing.net
Printed in the United States

To our kiddos,
Don't stop pursuing your dreams.
–Dad

Mommy loves you!
–Mom

To my wife and coauthor, Kayti.
You are my pillar and inspiration. I love you.

To my husband and his 1 percent.
I am happy to be your plus one.

ACKNOWLEDGMENTS

A special shoutout to Alexandra Weller for her lovely concept illustrations.

Our heartfelt thanks to Heather Koonce for reviewing the manuscript and assisting in editing.

Much appreciation to Curt Locklear and Melisa Graham for their editing.

Additional thanks to those who supported the writing of this book including Frankie Weller, Michael Weller, Steve Sulkin, Terrence Koonce, Brent Cook, Tricia Collom, and Kristina Abbruzzese.

Finally, our ongoing gratitude to the wonderful Warren Publishing team.

PROLOGUE
A DISTANT PAST

The Zuren transport ship *Gideon* swerved through a debris field, remnants of a planet once bustling with life. Sheathed in black thermal protective coating, the *Gideon* reflected no light, giving it the appearance of a dark rectangular void in space. It was racing away from a fiery battle in which the *Executer*, a Zuren megacraft, was holding off unknown attackers. The *Executer* had one mission: ensure the *Gideon* escaped, except this mission was compromised. Two Ipinidalans—multidimensional giants that could fly through the void without need of a vessel—had broken through the defenses to chase the *Gideon* and were firing electrostatic discharges at it.

The *Gideon* shuddered as a shot hit the bow. Inside, the two-man crew maintained their focus on outrunning their pursuers. In the copilot seat sat a tall, lanky Zuren humanoid with an oversized head. The pilot was a human, Captain Elton Blake, wearing the uniform of a nineteenth-century American naval officer. They had just deposited their cargo and were rushing to complete their final task.

"The *Executer* is taking major damage," the Zuren warned the pilot.

"I have the coordinates," Blake announced amidst a blast on the hull that brightened the cockpit. On all sides, the captain and his copilot had a full view of everything around them, using a technology that made the walls transparent from the inside.

"The Ipinidalans are gaining speed," the copilot announced. "Several Zuren ships are trying to intercede." Though humanlike, the Ipinidalans moved through space with speed and agility, starlight reflecting off their gold metallic armor. "They need more time!"

"I don't need your big head to tell me that!" the captain yelled, steering hard to port. "What's the status of the *Executer*?"

The copilot swept his hands across a fluidlike panel, revealing a rising red temperature gauge. "I'm reading a buildup in its nuclear core," he announced.

"That'll get the council's attention," Blake murmured, knowing this was part of the plan. The council he referred to was the Council of Nine, a governing body of the known universe who had outlawed the use of nuclear weapons.

"I'm really not sure this is a good idea," the Zuren warned.

"Would you like me to pull over, Sar?" Blake snapped. "This was your ridiculous idea!"

The *Executer* exploded in a bright flash of light. In response, the *Gideon*'s protective shield engaged, darkening the cockpit. The shock dampeners, which were designed to keep the body from experiencing the effects of sudden movements and acceleration, were damaged. Sar and Blake were thrown to the floor.

The alarms whirred, forcing Blake to cover his ears while he and Sar returned to their seats, but Blake tripped over a duffel bag that had been knocked loose. He shoved the bag to the side, then scrambled to the pilot's seat and frantically punched coordinates into the control panel. "There," he pointed to a stream of lights on the emergency viewscreen that projected from the navigation console.

Sar scanned the readout at his station, then raised his eyebrows. "The paradox," he said, pointing to a yellow screen. "It's happening!"

"I hope your plan works," Blake said, then tipped the ship into a wormhole that was now opening before them.

The Ipinidalans, undeterred by the oncoming paradox, followed the *Gideon*.

Blake and Sar could do nothing but grip their chairs while they traversed through time, space, and other dimensions. Though it felt to them like time stretched immeasurably, in mere seconds, the *Gideon* shot out of the wormhole. The Ipinidalans were on its tail, firing bolts of lightning at them from their war staffs. One of the shots sent the *Gideon* tumbling toward the blue-green planet known as Earth. The ship cracked under the fire of the pursuers, exposing the hull. The blast shields, still in place, protected its occupants, but the *Gideon*'s dampeners were damaged, throwing the pilot and his mate down and around the cockpit like shoes in a dryer.

Sar grasped the console while the captain bounced off the walls, swearing like a sailor. Sar pried the console open like clay, revealing its contents of loose wires. He grabbed two live wires and twisted them together, repairing the damage. Both he and the captain fell to the floor along with the precious duffel bag. "Dampeners are back on," he announced, shaking his throbbing hand.

"Thank you, Copilot Obvious," Blake muttered, rubbing his chin, sniffing the stench of burnt hair. He raised his head to see the planet grow rapidly as the ship plummeted toward the surface. It crashed in a meadow, tossing up dirt and forming a crater.

After a few moments, Sar reached for his companion. "Are you all right?" he asked.

"Did it work?" Blake asked.

Sar nodded. "The paradox sealed the access to the egg. The only way to open the door is with those," he said, pointing to the bag.

Shaken up after having been battered around like a paddle ball, the two men deactivated the emergency shields, flooding the cockpit with sunlight.

"We'll have to hide them, then" Blake said, grabbing the bag.

Sar coughed and wiped bright red blood from his forehead. A wall panel beeped softly with a blinking red light. He tapped the panel. At first, it was a blank screen. Then after a few seconds, green lights started to appear. "Looks like the Zuren ships following us made it," he said, pointing to the lights.

"Well, if they made it …," Blake said, then activated the viewscreen where the two Ipinidalan giants marched toward the ship, their staffs in hand. Blake recognized them as Scipio and Capriscas, two brothers known for their voracious lust for violence. The laws of physics did not apply to them. To many in the universe, the Ipinidalans were gods. To Blake, they were blood-thirsty, power-loving nuisances that posed a threat to intergalactic peace.

Their eyes sparkled yellow and blue as they glowered at the ship. The foremost one, Capriscas, towered over the wrecked ship, standing four times higher than a human. The giant peered into the cracked openings of the *Gideon*, sniffed, then with a swift thrust, jammed his staff into the cockpit through the viewscreen. The staff, brushing past Sar and Blake, crushed the panel behind them.

"Where are they?" the first giant yelled, kicking the ship.

Sar leaned over and whispered. "We're trapped!"

"No duh," Blake growled. "Again, with the obvious."

"Come out now, and we will make it easy on you," Scipio said, aiming his staff at the crashed vessel.

Blake, lying on the floor by Sar and holding on to the bag, lifted his head to make eye contact with Scipio. "How you doin', Skippy?" Blake asked, unable to resist taunting the giant.

Scipio grunted.

Blake ripped open the bag, revealing the four scrolls with silklike parchments. Sar shook his head in warning, but Blake ignored him. The captain grabbed one of the scrolls and muttered, "Kantara!" He immediately felt the power of the scroll surge through his body. He lifted his face to gaze into Sar's eyes, then smiled and winked.

***

Far into the Future

Moti stood alone and naked in the quiet darkness. Raising his hand a mere inch from his face, he could see nothing. Discouraged, he dropped his arm, soundlessly slapping his bare thigh. Somehow the lack of sound muted the sensation of the slap. He had visited this realm between dimensions several times before, but it still unsettled him. This realm was not created for human beings.

"Scipio!" Moti called—or tried to. His call merely vibrated on his lips and died. No matter; *intention* is what mattered in this place.

The hair on Moti's skin prickled as a cool breeze brushed by him and the sound of wind reached his ears. Light peeked in, exposing the outline of a shadowy humanoid ahead.

"Yes," acknowledged the ominous being, opening luminescent eyes that sparkled yellow and blue. Scipio was an Ipinidalan, the multidimensional beings tasked to serve as time sentinels. He brought light and sound with him into the void.

Unafraid, Moti addressed the large figure. "The Council of Nine sent me."

Scipio gave a curt nod, then raised his left hand. Moti's clothes returned to his body. First was the protection of the black shoes, then his dark-blue cloak, emblematic of a Council of Nine member. The light-blue slacks came last, blocking the breeze to his nether regions. Moti was sure this was Scipio's way of debasing him since Moti descended from a long line of aristocracy.

Scipio materialized into an ominous figure covered with white cloth and the iconic Ipinidalan metallic armor lined in gleaming gold. He held a spear in his hand. Moti, dwarfed by Scipio, estimated that if they stood side by side, Moti might be able to touch Scipios's knee.

The giant walked forward, shrinking with each step, and then stopped a few feet away from Moti. The yellow and blue still blazed from the sentinel's eyes, but his face showed no expression.

"What is the council's request?" Scipio asked, now with the voice of a mortal man.

"I need you to open the timeline backwards," Moti answered, spreading both arms apart with a nonchalant gesture.

"It is forbidden for you to travel back in time. Did you forget that you are prisoners to your timeline?" the Ipinidalan asked, pointing a finger at Moti.

"I'm not talking about moving through other timelines, just our own," Moti countered.

Scipio's eyes widened with interest. "You've figured out how to prevent a paradox?"

"Yes." Moti rubbed his hands together. "Nobody else will know but me and the doctor," he reassured the sentinel. "After all, I'm on the council." Moti gave Scipio a smoldering smile. "I am the council," he added.

Scipio's spear shrunk into a cane, and the Ipinidalan leaned onto it, cautiously considering how to reply now that he knew Moti was acting on his own, not with the support or the knowledge of the rest of the council. "The scrolls," Scipio said excitedly, but then realized Moti's intention. "You're talking about war."

"I'm talking about freedom for all of us," Moti said. "We will need your help, which means you will need the scrolls."

"What is your plan?" Scipio asked, intrigued with Moti's proposition.

"We will send someone from the twenty-first century to the Second Age where the first scroll resides. Once he has the scroll in hand, we will then connect him with the captain," Moti explained with assurance.

Scipio twisted his face in disgust at the mention of the captain. "Of course. It always comes back to that damn captain."

Moti straightened his back with confidence. "I ran all the scenarios," Moti reassured, "and this is the only one with any promise of success."

The Ipinidalan closed his eyes, twirling the cane while he contemplated scenarios of his own, but his conclusions matched Moti's. "I agree," Scipio conceded, opening his eyes, which were now completely black. "Bring me all four scrolls, and you will get your war." Scipio stopped spinning his cane and thrust it into the ground.

"I see you're still fond of your old man stick," Moti said, noting that Scipio never parted with his cane.

Scipio squinted, contemplating the meaning of Moti's words.

"Judging by your silence, we can proceed then?" Moti asked, tightening his fists with anticipation.

Scipio's cane transformed to a staff. Lightning struck it with a deafening thunder. Moti covered his ears and shut his eyes. Wind blew through Moti's hair, then steadied into a soft breeze. He opened his eyes to see an infinite stream of lights that split like the roots of a tree at both ends. Crossing through the middle was a bright, tightly wound tube that Moti recognized as the representation of his timeline.

"There's your tunnel," Scipio said, exhaling.

"I will let the doctor know," Moti said, watching the formation of lights dance before him.

"When you find the captain, be cautious," Scipio warned. "He's the only pathetic mortal to ever kill an Ipinidalan." Scipio sneered, revealing jagged white teeth.

Moti hung his head with bewilderment. "All the power of time and space," Moti said, "and yet a mere mortal can still be such a threat to you."

"Nevertheless, I will have to kill him," Scipio warned.

Not wanting to argue, Moti let the warning dissipate. "I can't answer to that." Moti spun around, his cloak swirling behind him, then walked briskly away. Without stopping, he spoke over his shoulder. "I will let you know when we have the first scroll."

A portal resembling a pool of rippling water opened before Moti. "Don't let me down, Keiji," he murmured to himself.

PART I

CHAPTER 1

Liquid pressed against me from all sides and from within, my lungs heavy and tight. I felt like an embryo moving around in my mother's womb. I heard the ping of what sounded like a sonar echo, then I collapsed to the ground, water splashing over me.

I coughed up liquid, then gasped for air. I rolled over, clawing at the ground, but it gave way beneath me like mud after a rainstorm. I slid onto the burning surface of a desert floor. I tried to stand but was unable to move my legs. Suddenly, fatigue overtook me, and I fell into the darkness of sleep.

"Keiji," whispered a man's voice. "Wake up."

I opened my eyes, blocking the sun with my hand, then gazed at my surroundings, unsure where I was or how long I had been unconscious. Flat sand and rock ran nearly to the horizon, with rolling foothills just barely visible beyond. Beneath me was a bed of crumbling rock and dirt cracked like eggshells. Beside me was a lump of dirt and wilted grass. The hot, dry air smelled only of dust.

Where am I?

"Keiji," called the voice again. I struggled to my feet, searching for the source.

"Who's there?" I demanded, gazing around, but only spotting a dust devil racing across the desert floor.

"I am a doctor," the disembodied voice answered.

The last thing I remembered was walking home from work, crossing a grassy park that led to my apartment. I was now standing in a desert, hearing a bodiless voice call out to me. This wasn't a dream. I was here, wherever this place was. "Am I dead?" I asked out loud, wondering if that was the explanation for my lack of concern. *What else could it be?*

"No, thank goodness," the voice answered.

On instinct, I raised my tone. "Then what's going on?" I asked, still unsure to whom I was speaking.

"You took a little trip," the voice informed me.

"Was I drugged?" I murmured, gazing at the wind-worn rock formations in the distance. One of the rocks was shaped like a needle.

"In a way, yes," the voice answered. "You were just transported back in time in a sort of biodegradable bubble. The fluid you were covered with works like a sedative."

I turned around to see if anyone was standing nearby. With a clear view of my surroundings on all sides, there was no doubt that I was alone, with only the eye of the desert sun on my body. The voice existed only in my head. "Back in time, eh?" I said, not sure if I should be alarmed.

The bleached ground reflected the sunlight, so I removed my jacket and held it over my head to provide some shade. The jacket sleeve rubbed across the back of my head, and I felt a twinge of pain. I reached around and noticed a small mosquito-bite-sized bump, but the pain penetrated my skull, like a needle insertion. The twinge of pain subsided within seconds, but the small bump remained.

"Okay, I'll play along." I amused myself with the imaginary voice in my head, scanning the terrain for any shelter, such as a cave. "How far back in time?" I asked. I was unable to see anything promising, so I walked down a dried-up riverbed to continue my search for shelter and, if possible, some water.

"You've traveled back in time to what we call the Second Age," the voice claimed with a soft tone, like that of a history professor rambling off facts of no interest to any of the students.

I heard the words but didn't fully comprehend them since my immediate concern was survival. "What's the Second Age?" I asked.

"It's the second age of human civilization," the doctor muttered.

I spotted a cliff face, able to see shade below, and I walked toward it. "Okay, Doctor," I uttered with acceptance.

I reached the shade, relieved to relax my eyes from the blinding sun, but the heat remained. I laid my jacket on the ground, unbuttoned the cuffs of my shirt, and rolled up my sleeves. I slapped the dirt off my jeans and removed the pebbles from my running shoes, then sat down. "Why am I here?"

"You should rest," the voice advised, not answering my question. "The trip you took wears down the human body."

Taking the advice from the doctor, or whoever he was, I leaned against the rocks of the cliff. I took an inventory of what was around me, letting my mind race with memories of my father, specifically the trip we took to Death Valley. He enjoyed it, but all I remembered was being hot. My eyes fixed on the formation of stones before me, which were now under the protective shade of the cliff. The stones were not a natural formation. They were stacked there, maybe to serve as a marker or a warning to others.

"You're a doctor, eh?" I asked, wiping the sweat and dust gathering on my forehead.

"That is what I'm called," the doctor confirmed.

"No name, like Bob," I snickered, repositioning myself, trying to get comfortable.

Without elaboration, the voice responded, "No, just call me 'doctor.'"

I rested my head in my hands, watching heat waves rise from the formation of stones still exposed to the sun. My eyelids felt heavy from trying to block the bright sunlight that reflected off the ground. I closed my eyes and let my mind take me to wherever dreams awaited.

This dream led me to a work cubicle where I sat typing out a request to my boss for time off to spend with my father. I sent the message off, then felt someone squeeze my shoulder. I spun around to face my father, who held the request I just sent to my boss. I hugged him, closing my eyes. When I opened them again, I was standing in the middle of the living room at my grandmother's house. It was no longer my father I was hugging but, rather, my mother, sobbing with a crumpled newspaper in her hand. I grabbed the paper and smoothed it out so I could read it. It was a picture of my father under a headline mentioning his recent death. My father stepped out of the paper, standing before me, holding his hand up, not wanting me to step any closer. "Wake up," he whispered, but with the voice of the doctor.

I stirred in my sleep but felt myself step out from the dreamworld slowly to the reality that lay before me.

"Wake up, Keiji," the doctor repeated.

I slowly opened my eyes to see only darkness, and I was shivering. The cold desert night had crept in while I slept.

"Are you rested?" he asked.

"Yes, but I'm cold and thirsty." I coughed with the sensation that my throat and mouth had turned to sandpaper. I felt my jacket beside me and put it on.

I looked up at the velvety black night sky, with twinkling stars amid a vast universe. The star constellations seemed different, like they were closer. Also, something was missing.

"Where's the moon?" I asked, assuming it hadn't risen yet, but not sure, and happy to engage in any conversation that would take my mind off the cold.

"There is no moon," the doctor answered with a congratulatory tone.

Not believing the doctor, I scanned the entire sky, but still, no moon was in sight. "Seriously, where is the moon?"

"It's not there yet," the doctor answered.

I tucked my hands into my armpits, hoping to warm them. I was too cold to think about what the doctor meant. "Where are you?" I asked through chattering teeth, hoping the doctor would miraculously appear with a hot drink and a blanket.

"I'm talking to you from the future," the doctor replied, then paused. I heard clicking in the background as if the doctor were punching buttons. "I need you to get up and start moving around to produce some body heat."

In obeisance, I sprinted in place to generate warmth, hearing keys rattle in my pocket. I reached for my keys to pull them out. To my delight, I also felt a pocket lighter.

It was my father's, and I carried it with me wherever I went. Never used it because I didn't smoke, but my father did, and it reminded me of him. I pulled out the lighter and spun the flint wheel. A flame flickered before my eyes. *It worked!* I flipped the lid shut, snuffing out the flame, not wanting to waste the lighter fluid. I patted my back pockets in search for my cell phone, but it was missing. I searched the area with my hands, but I could not find it. I gave up, deciding to focus on more important matters.

I left the area in search of kindling and firewood or whatever most resembled it in this desert. Rocks shifted under my feet while I stumbled along in the dark.

Neither water nor warmth was within grasp for the first hour. I listened for any signs of life, like the scampering of an animal or the howl of a coyote. I heard nothing but the constant ringing in my ears from shooting rifles as a kid with my uncles. They didn't believe in earplugs.

Starlight revealed the silhouette of a leafless tree. I pulled on a branch, and it snapped off with ease, so I broke off several more. I collected some twigs and dry grass to start a fire with my lighter. Within minutes, I warmed my hands against the yellow flames of burning wood.

"Are you feeling better?" the doctor asked, somehow aware of my activities.

"I'm warming up, but I'm thirsty. I'll be okay though. Why am I here?" I asked, wondering if I'd asked the question before.

"I need you to find something and bring it back to me," the doctor said.

"Why not get it yourself?" I asked.

"Sending you is much easier," the doctor admitted.

"And why am I not panicking right now?" I asked.

"Humans have a wonderful ability to adapt," the doctor answered. "Also, the sedative hasn't fully worn off yet."

I grunted at the answer. "What are you sending me to find?" I asked, feeling like I was repeating myself.

"A scroll," the doctor stated bluntly.

"A scroll?" I was now experiencing a sensation that could only be described as annoyance associated with being baffled by something that sounded completely ridiculous. "Where is it?" I asked, sitting cross-legged on the ground.

"Nobody is completely sure, but we believe that Ganteep City may hold a clue to its whereabouts," the doctor theorized.

"Feels like a fool's errand," I admitted out loud, but the doctor did not respond or find it offensive. "I've never heard of such a city," I said, thinking about my frequent travels around the globe growing up.

My father served in the United States military. He met my mother when he was stationed overseas. I enjoyed traveling and visiting new places. My mother and I visited family in her hometown of Kokura, Japan every year until I went to college. I considered myself to be a world traveler, but I had never heard of anything that sounded remotely like "Ganteep."

"That knowledge has been lost to you and your time, but I assure you it exists," the doctor said.

"How do I get to this Ganteep City?" I asked, not caring to argue but slightly offended by the doctor's curt answer.

"I've tracked someone not too far from you who is heading your way, probably having spotted your fire," the doctor said. "Stay where you are, and your paths should cross."

"Can I trust him?" I asked, suddenly feeling vulnerable and thinking the fire was probably not a wise move since it likely just announced my location to anyone in the surrounding area.

"I hope so," the doctor muttered.

I winced at the doctor's answer—his plan didn't seem very well thought out. I relaxed my mind and focused on something else. "What is Ganteep City like?" I asked, with vivid images swirling through my mind of ancient civilizations with pillars, obelisks, and pyramids.

The doctor softened his tone. "I hear it is beautiful."

Suddenly tired, I fell asleep watching the flames dancing before me.

CHAPTER 2
DAWN OF THE SECOND DAY

I awoke shivering. My campfire was reduced to embers and ash. The heat from the rising sun, however, promised another scorching day with only a slight breeze. I stood scanning the horizon for the person whom the doctor mentioned, thoughts racing through my mind. *What did he look like? What would he say? Would he attack?*

Spasms in my calves and thighs forced me to grab my legs and rub them with what little energy I had left. Fatigue quickly set in again, and I sat down in the shade of the rocks to preserve energy while waiting for an uncertain future. I hunched over to lie on my side and listened to the wheezing of my breath.

A lake formed in the desert, giving me the promise of water to quench my thirst. It took every ounce of my strength to stand. Wobbly at first, I stepped toward the water, but it eluded me. I quickened my pace, but all I found was cracked earth. The mirage was replaced by the sun-bleached bones of a four-legged animal that once roamed the area. Hope drained from my mind, replaced by confusion as I tried to comprehend my surroundings and situation.

My knees collapsed, and I sank to the ground. Dazed, I watched the mirage once again beckon me to creep forward, but my legs refused to comply. Lightheaded, I wanted to drift away into nothingness. The ground seemed to rise, and unconsciousness overtook me once more.

I have no idea how long I slept. When I awoke, my skin felt dry, and my muscles twitched under the sun's constant barrage. I breathed in deeply, but instead of air, there was only dust. I coughed and choked as my body fought for a clean breath. I blinked, and through the dust I saw a figure with a spear approaching. My mouth gaped open to call out, but like a switch, darkness replaced the light.

And again, I dreamed.

A gentle lap of water from the lake hit the shoreline, depositing driftwood. The peaty smell of algae filled my nose. I sat on a beach and dug into the sand to reach the moist layers below. Once a hole was dug, I planted my feet in it and fisted my toes, then filled the hole with sand over my feet, burying and cooling them.

Swimmers splashed water into each other's faces, talking and laughing while the roar of boats thumped across the wakes of other boats. One of the swimmers, whom I recognized as my dad, shook water off his hair. His gray eyes were unmistakable. He waved at me with excitement, insisting I join in the fun. I wanted to join them, but my body refused any commands to move.

My feet started to burn in the sand. I tried to pull them out, but the sand held me down as if I were stuck in dried cement. I lifted my head up to call for help from my father, but instead, he grimaced.

Taking pity, my dad slapped water at me from the lake, but the water dissipated in the air before it could reach me. He furrowed his brow and slapped again with the same effect. Making a sour face, my dad twisted his torso and slapped the water with extra force, but the water still fell short of reaching me.

With a softened face, my dad cupped his hand into the water and, without leaving the lake, held his hands out to me and poured water over my face. The water flowed from his hand, but it did not penetrate my lips. My dad frowned, then with a sinister grin, whispered in my ear. "We'll have to do this the hard way," he said, then jammed his hand into my mouth, and water began pouring in.

I coughed, waking up to someone hunched over, holding my head to the side and pouring water across my lips. I coughed again and heard my companion speak, but the words were foreign to me.

I opened my eyes to see a woman's figure casting a shadow over me, which I welcomed since it blocked the scorching sun. She tilted her head, and all I saw was her striking green eyes that glowed even in the brightness. A thin scar extended from her left brow, over her eye and down to her cheekbone.

She spoke, but I could not understand her. She bit her lower lip in contemplation, then lifted me up to a sitting position and placed a pouch with a nozzle into my hand. I held the pouch to my mouth and chugged the warm water.

After a few gulps, she retrieved her pouch and held up her hand, warning me to stop drinking. She helped me to stand and escorted me back to where I had prepared a fire the night before. I rested, regaining my strength, listening to her talk, but was still unable to understand her. She carried on with her activities, speaking at random without expecting an answer from me.

The shade and water helped me to regain my senses, but I was not strong enough to stand on my own yet. She was taller than me and wearing skins, belts, and straps. A quiver of arrows and a bow were slung over her back. On her right side, an ax was tucked into a belt. A spear lay on the desert floor.

Again she spoke, and again I could not interpret her words.

"I don't understand what you are saying," I said with a dry mouth, frustrated.

"Be silent!" The doctor's voice startled me.

"Why?" I asked. The woman snapped around, observing me.

"I'm troubleshooting something," the doctor said.

With lips pursed, I remained silent. The newcomer took a seat on a rock across from me, grasping on to her spear. She watched me without talking.

"Okay. I need her to speak to you now," the doctor said.

"What do you want me to do?" I responded with annoyance.

The woman spoke and lowered her spear.

"Keep talking to her," the doctor encouraged.

I wondered if she thought I was crazy for speaking to someone else who was not physically present. "Hi," I greeted, holding out my arm, then placed my hand on my chest. "I'm Keiji."

She muttered various phrases, but I heard one word distinctly— *who!*

"Who," I repeated, and she twitched in shock as if in sudden comprehension. "What's going on?" I questioned the doctor.

"Your brain has been programmed to translate what others say," the doctor explained.

"What do you mean?" I asked. She widened her eyes.

"Your brain is learning her language, and when it does, you will be able to speak with her. Your mind can also project a telepathic field that will translate your words into the language she understands," the doctor explained, trying unsuccessfully to hide the enthusiasm in his voice.

"That's incredible," I marveled.

"You will have to remain in proximity for it to work," the doctor added. "It will be awkward for you at first because there is a slight delay between the time the other person speaks and the time you hear what is said. The lips won't match what you hear, so don't speak so fast."

"Oh!" I exclaimed. "Like those foreign films with English dubbed in." I remember the old kung fu movies where the people mouthed the words in their native tongues, but someone recorded the words in English. It was the subject of several comedy acts in my time.

"I have no idea what you're talking about," the doctor said, giving me the impression that he did but had a dry sense of humor.

"Who," she repeated. The word she mouthed did not match what I heard.

"Who," I said, repeating it for her. She scrunched her nose and leaned in to inspect my lips.

"Who," she repeated back, so I kept up the charade until her lips turned upward into a smile.

"Who are you?" I asked, suddenly feeling like an owl after repeating "who."

My companion jolted her head back in surprise. She tucked stray hairs behind her ear, then put her hand on her chest. "Hazi," she said, both word and mouth spoken in perfect synchronization.

"Hazi," I repeated, licking my upper lip. I whispered to the doctor. "How come there is no delay when she says Hazi?"

"Because there is no translation for that word. I believe that is her name," the doctor guessed.

I held out my hand, pointing to her. "Hazi," I said, then put my hand to my chest, "Keiji."

"Keiji," she repeated.

My heart skipped a beat. I was communicating with her! "Thank you for helping me," I said with gratitude, being sure to speak slowly and clearly.

Her mouth moved, and a second later her voice reached my ears. "Don't mention it."

CHAPTER 3
AFTERNOON

A shadow zipped by us, which drew Hazi's attention upward. I surveyed the sky to seek the source of the shadow but found nothing. Hazi, on the other hand, spotted something right away, dropped her spear and ax, and with her bow in hand, ran in hot pursuit. An hour later, hoping she hadn't befallen an accident and left me for dead, I was relieved when she returned holding a bird with an arrow through its body. The bird was the size of a large hawk, covered in white feathers with a brown head.

"Hungry?" she asked. She pulled the arrow out, wiped off the blood, then returned it to her quiver. Bracing the bird with one hand, she pulled at the feathers and cleaned it. I stared, entranced with her level of efficiency.

The sun glowed orange, snuggling beneath the horizon to rest for the night. I collected dried logs and started another fire. "I didn't think I'd find this much wood in a desert," I admitted.

"Wasn't always a desert," she replied, skewering the bird on her spear, then propped it over the fire.

"How did you find me?" I asked

"Last night, I saw your fire glowing, so I headed your way."

Lighting a fire in the open for all to see was probably not the smartest thing to do. I cringed at the thought that I could have been a victim to a ruthless cutthroat. "I'm lucky you found me."

The flame flickered, casting shadows onto Hazi's face. Dust covered her body, but I could make out a thin layer of hair on her legs and arms. She didn't shave, nor did she need to. There was perfection in her shape and skin tone. Despite the ruggedness of her appearance, she was attractive.

"I've heard rumors of people who can understand and speak different tongues," she postulated, pointing to my head with the skewered bird. "I haven't ever met anyone with that ability, though." She readjusted herself. "Nice outfit, by the way," she kidded, reminding me that my clothes were out of both time and place.

"You don't seem surprised or bothered by me," I said, watching her flip the bird to make sure it was properly cooked on all sides.

Hazi wrinkled her forehead, then sighed. "Fantastic things happen all the time, but you," she began, raising an eyebrow, "you are a curiosity. Why are you here?"

"It's okay," the doctor reassured. "Talk to her freely."

Heeding the doctor's advice, I answered her question. "I need to go to Ganteep City," I hesitated, "to recover a scroll."

Hazi narrowed her eyes. "Just walk in and grab a scroll, eh?"

"It is an important scroll," I contended.

"Who's in your head?" Hazi asked, pressing her finger against her temple.

I was unsure of what to say.

The doctor chimed in. "Talk to her so she can trust you. You have an empathic field emanating from your mind, which means she will be able to sense if you are lying, so just be honest."

Resting my elbows on my knees, I steepled my fingers. "He calls himself 'doctor.' All I know is that he's from the future."

"Where are you from?" she asked as she pulled out her ax, cut into the bird, checked it, then put it back over the fire.

"I believe I'm from the future too," I admitted.

Hazi pressed her lips in a straight line, focusing on roasting her bird. "I'm guessing humans haven't changed much in the future, biologically speaking," she humored.

"In my time, some people suggest humans have only been around a few thousand years," I reminisced, recalling the many conversations at school and church where we speculated about civilizations in the distant past.

Clearing her throat, Hazi extended the bird farther into the fire. My mouth watered with the smell of the roast before me. I flexed my hands at the thought of holding such a large bird for so long. Her strength clearly surpassed mine.

The sun had set, and the stars were speckled across the sky. For me, one important light was missing. "I wonder what happened to the moon?"

"Moon?" she asked. "This planet does not have one."

"What do you mean?" I asked.

"This planet has never had a moon," she stated.

"That's interesting," I murmured, then watched her cook the bird in silence. Her hands were steady, and I allowed my eyes to travel upward to inspect her attire. Her hair had several braids tied off with leather straps, extending past her shoulders. My eyes followed the braids leading down to her chest.

Her movement stopped, and I quickly shifted my gaze back up to see her staring back at me. I blushed.

"Doctor, are you there?" I beckoned with a whisper, wanting to divert Hazi's attention.

"Just listening to your heart race," the doctor humored.

It was apparent the doctor was somehow monitoring me, much like a lab rat. "How much can she sense?" I asked, covering my mouth.

"The empathic field does convey a range of emotion, but it really only magnifies emotions related to deceit or trust," the doctor elaborated. "The empathic field goes both ways, but it is very limited, to allow you some privacy." The doctor paused. "I think."

Only slightly relieved, I lifted my head to make eye contact with Hazi. She spread a grin on her face.

"You *think*?" I growled to the doctor. "What do you mean by that?"

Hazi hunched over, pressing her elbows against her knees. "You do know that I can hear everything you are saying to the doctor, don't you?" Her face beamed with humor.

The blood drained from my face. I buried my head in my knees, listening to the fire crackle, mad at myself for being so stupid and scolding myself for acting like a teenage boy.

Once the blood returned to my head, I unburied myself. "What are you doing in this place? Are you from here?" I questioned, desperate to change the subject.

"I've been exploring these lands," she said. With her free hand, she waved it toward the open lands behind me. "This is the site of a great battle. Nuclear weapons left this place a barren wasteland."

"How long ago?" I asked.

"The battle happened a few years before I was born," she said, brushing a braid behind her shoulder.

Hazi did not appear much older than me. If this place had been nuked so recently, had I been exposed to radiation? I broke out in a cold sweat. "I'm guessing you're twenty-five years old, so isn't there still radiation fallout?" I spoke with naivety.

She smiled. "Wait, what?" she grimaced. "The attack was well over two centuries ago, and the danger of the fallout only lasted maybe five years."

I threw out the book of etiquette in my mind. "How old are you?" I asked, having never asked a woman her age ever.

"Two hundred twenty-six," she answered.

I bit my upper lip. Here was a woman who looked to be my age, when in fact she was more than ten times older than me. *Maybe she measures years differently than I do?*

The doctor sensed my reasoning. "She is," the doctor said.

"She is what?" I asked. Hazi tilted her head in curiosity at my conversation with my invisible companion.

"Two hundred twenty-six years old," the doctor confirmed. "People lived much longer back then."

Feeling betrayed by my circumstances, I reacted back. "I might live to be eighty, and she is already more than a century older than that?"

"Yes," the doctor affirmed. "By the way, Keiji, you can communicate with me using telepathy," he said in a matter-of-fact tone. "You don't have to speak, but be intentional in what you want to say; otherwise, I will only receive the ramblings of jumbled thoughts."

I rolled my eyes. "Now he tells me."

Hazi shook her head, exposing her perfectly white teeth, finding my predicament humorous. She inspected the bird. "You're just a baby then," she kidded, then handed me a piece of meat using an arrow as a skewer. I took it.

I rested the arrow on my knee to give my dinner some time to cool. I massaged the back of my neck, feeling the bump. "How long do you live?" I asked Hazi as she bit into her dinner.

She finished chewing. "Let's just say that some live thousands of years," she answered.

"Wow!" My jaw hung open.

Hazi shifted her weight, bringing her legs together. "So you're here to find a scroll," she inquired, then took another bite. "I'll help you."

"Excellent," the doctor exclaimed in my head.

I breathed a sigh of relief. "Thank you." I tested the temperature of my food with my finger. Satisfied, I took a bite. The meat tasted like turkey.

"Don't thank me too soon," she warned. "The people of Ganteep won't exactly welcome me."

CHAPTER 4

Tired and drowsy, I rose from my slumber with an aching body from sleeping on hard, cold, and unforgiving ground. All around me was the familiar arid, lifeless desert. I stretched and, with a surge of energy, leaped to my feet and marched up a small hill to get a better view of the landscape. I raked my fingers through my hair with an uneasy feeling. I was alone.

Discouraged, I looked over my shoulder to the campfire and noticed Hazi's quiver placed neatly on the ground. I exhaled with relief when I saw her step out from behind a boulder.

"Where were you?" I asked, trying not to sound needy.

"What do you do when you wake up?" she asked.

I grinned, then decided to follow her example and relieve myself. A half hour later, we trekked together across the desert.

My thoughts about our destination kept me occupied at first but gave way to the aches in my feet and body. The doctor chimed in rarely, though I sensed his presence constantly.

Signs of life increased the farther we marched on. A dog-sized lizard scurried to a rock, stopped, blinked, and stared at us. Its head followed our movements while we passed.

Hazi maintained a steady pace, showing no concern for any danger. Several times I gazed upon her body and movements. Much of her arms and legs were exposed, giving me a good view of her tanned, toned, and smooth skin. Her muscle striations were visible with the flex of each step. I, on the other hand, needed to hit the gym if I ever wanted to add muscle to my scrawny body.

Hazi halted and adjusted her belt, exposing a thin but lengthy scar that extended vertically up her thigh.

I pulled up my jacket sleeve to examine my own scar on my forearm. I got this badge while riding my bike as a young kid. A car struck me, throwing me from my bike into its hood. The antenna broke off and sliced my arm open. I got lucky that day, but the scar was a constant reminder of my mortality.

I stumbled over a rock and nearly twisted my ankle, bringing my attention to the present.

We stopped to rest at a boulder that towered over us, providing some shade. I welcomed the rest while we hydrated and wiped the sweat from our brows. We sat facing the direction from which we came. I heard what I thought was the rustling of trees but dismissed the noise as the effect of fatigue and heat.

"Near the campsite," I began, "by the cliff was a formation of rocks. I wonder why it was built."

"Probably a marker for travelers or a warning that a wasteland is ahead," she said. Her speculation was comparably like a sign on a highway, informing the driver that the next gas station is over a hundred miles away. "Let me show you something teeming with life." She beckoned me to follow her with the wave of her hand. We rounded the boulder and hiked upward until we halted atop a cliff, overlooking a forest.

Birds rode a steady wind above tall trees that seemed to brush the sky. In the distance, rising cliffs gave way to waterfalls cascading from their edges.

"Oh wow," I murmured, admiring the plunging water and the rainbows that rose above.

Hazi clutched her water pouch, lifting it and pointing forward beyond the waterfalls. "Ganteep City is in that direction."

She gave me the pouch, and I took a drink from our rapidly depleting water source. I handed the nearly empty pouch back to Hazi and pointed to the tree line. "Why does the forest start suddenly as if on an invisible line?"

"After the war, the Ganteep people worked to make this land capable of supporting life again," she explained. "They began with their oasis, which has been expanding ever since."

Describing the land as an oasis was an understatement, and the work of the Ganteep people to cultivate this land was nothing short of miraculous. "Are they peaceful?" I asked.

Hazi gave me a smirk. "They can be, but they are also self-serving with many prejudices."

I sighed, disappointed. "Against whom?" I asked.

"Outsiders in general, but they have a particular disdain for giants," she said.

"Giants?" I asked. "Like really big people?"

Hazi nodded.

"Where did they come from?" I asked.

Hazi hooked the water pouch onto her belt. "Those from above mated with women, who bore giants," she explained. "Many giants live in the Land of Darmant."

"Who are the ones from above?" I asked, looking skyward.

Hazi thought for a moment. "Some people from the stars," she said with no further explanation. Hazi rose to her feet and grabbed her spear. "Let's go and see if we can make it to the waterfalls by noon."

We skidded down a hill, crossed through some vegetation, and approached the forest line. I was astonished to see very little underbrush, which gave me hope that walking through the forest was going to be relatively pleasant, like walking through Central Park in New York City.

We stepped into the forest and immediately found a trail leading in the direction of the waterfalls. Tree roots twisted across the pathway, but other than that, the forest floor was clear of leaves and rocks—no more fear of slipping and twisting my ankle.

About a hundred yards into the forest, animal life flourished. Squirrels scurried up and down trees, and rabbits playfully hopped around in the grass exposed to the sunlight.

A single buck crossed our path, paying us no attention as it grazed. It was larger than any buck I'd seen, with an antler rack towering from its skull. The massive beast popped its head up, suddenly spooked, then with elegance and strength, bolted into a full sprint. A mob of deer followed him, leaping across the trail.

I gasped. "That's a big buck!"

"They make for good eating," she said quietly, pulling out her bow with a heightened level of vigilance.

"Is that our dinner tonight?" I asked, half joking.

"It is illegal to hunt here," she warned, scanning her surroundings.

A raucous noise to our left grabbed our attention. Amidst the rustling of leaves and crashing limbs, a spear flew over our heads. "Ha!" bellowed a low voice.

Hazi shoved me behind one of the bushes near the trail, where my face became engulfed in spiderwebs. In a panic, I clawed at my face to remove them. Hazi slapped her hand onto my mouth, silencing me. I fought the urge to make any noise as images of spiders crawling across my face filled my head.

The thud of a footstep hit the ground near us, then another. About a dozen thuds later, I saw him. A giant wearing a white wool shirt and pants made of deerskins stepped onto the trail and sniffed the air, brushing his hair from his face. He was perfectly proportioned to a human, just bigger.

Turning his head side to side, the giant peered through the trees, looking for his kill. Spotting it, he trotted forward, then reached for his spear and raised it up to show an impaled buck. He gripped the animal by its legs and ripped it off his spear, clanging antlers against a nearby tree.

"Did you see that?" I whispered to the doctor, not expecting a response.

"I did," the doctor said with apparent awe.

The giant snapped his gaze to the side, sensing danger, then was knocked backward by what appeared to be a tranquilizer dart that produced an electrical shock. The giant jolted upright and dropped his prey, shuddering with pain. Appearing rattled, he grabbed his head but then was jolted again by another whisking dart. His eyes rolled to the back of his head, knees buckled, and he collapsed to the ground unconscious.

"Secured," reported a man stepping out from the brush. He was wearing a helmet and a beige uniform and carrying a weapon with a magazine protruding from the side. Unlike Hazi and the giant, who wore skins and appeared to descend from hunters and gatherers, this newcomer had the appearance of a futuristic warrior from some far-off place. The gun resembled a 9-millimeter Lanchester submachine gun that was once a prized possession of my father. Several soldiers stepped out in the open, wearing the same kind of attire and carrying identical weapons. "Call in a lift, and let's take him to the city," the first soldier ordered.

One of the other soldiers pointed his weapon in my direction. "We aren't alone," he warned, twirling his hand above his head. In response, they all raised their weapons and marched toward us.

The doctor screamed into my head, "Here they come!" I had no time to react before someone grabbed me from behind and pulled me out of hiding, quickly overpowering me. The same happened to Hazi, except she struck her assailant on the helmet with the blunt end of her spear, causing him to wobble and lose balance. Within seconds, he was lying on the ground moaning. With her bow, Hazi sent an arrow into my attacker, sending him flailing.

Another soldier aimed his weapon, but Hazi quickly shot an arrow at him, piercing his hand and knocking the weapon to the ground. She pointed a loaded bow at the remaining trooper, but anticipating her next move, he had already fired his weapon, hitting her with jolts of electricity.

I turned to assist Hazi.

"Look out!" screamed the doctor, but it was too late. Every atom in my body seemed to split apart as if I was hit by a lightning bolt. I saw a flash of light, then darkness.

***

I awoke to the potent stench of something placed under my nose. My wrists were bound, and I was lying on a patch of dirt. A medic was kneeling beside me. Dazed from a pounding headache, I raised my bound hands to my temples and rubbed them, hoping to alleviate the pain. The medic helped me sit upright, then checked me for injuries. Once satisfied all was okay, he left me to assist Hazi, who was also bound.

Also concerned about my safety was the doctor. "Are you okay?" he asked.

Other than a freaking massive headache, I thought, *I'm okay.*

A soldier with dark skin, short gray hair, and blue eyes approached me. His uniform was decked with accoutrements and braids along the seams of his jacket. His rifle-like weapon was slung across his back, and a sidearm pistol was holstered midway down his thigh. His dirty boots rose past his calves. He differed from the other soldiers, who had dark eyes and brown skin as if from Arabic descent.

He unhooked a wooden baton from his belt and jabbed it into my chest. "It is illegal to poach or hunt in these woods," he informed me.

"I didn't do either of those things," I defended, pushing the stick away. The soldier flinched, as if someone was trying to strike him. His mouth dropped with astonishment at the dubbing of my voice.

"Don't piss him off," the doctor warned.

What about me? I retorted. *I'm pretty pissed off!*

"Captain Malah," called a soldier from behind. The man before me turned to acknowledge him. "The giant is loaded on the conveyer and being taken to the city," he said.

The captain acknowledged the soldier's report with the wave of his hand and returned his attention to me.

"Captain Malah?" I asked, clarifying to be sure of his name.

With a sudden change of demeanor, the captain grinned, returned his baton to his belt, and without warning, manhandled me to my feet. I steadied myself as he brushed off the debris from my jacket and then slapped my arm, creating a cloud of dust and sending me into a coughing fit.

"You are a bit of a mystery, young man," Malah smirked. He gestured to a subordinate. "Looks like we found our anomaly," he said, then barked, "Take them!"

Chapter 5
MIDMORNING

The iron handcuffs dug into my wrists and weighed down my arms. Guards pushed us forward through the trees, taking a straight-line path away from the trails. Four soldiers kept their weapons trained on Hazi, staying a healthy distance from her, but only one guard accompanied me.

A grunt reverberated in my ears, startling me. I twisted around to pinpoint the source of the sound. "What was that?" I asked out loud.

The soldier with me answered. "Security of sorts," he assured, lifting his visor, then chuckled. I didn't feel very reassured.

We stepped out of the forest onto a meadow of grass covered with yellow wildflowers. Butterflies with purple wings fluttered in the sunlight while the sound of dragonflies buzzed in my ears. Under different circumstances this place would be enchanting—perfect for a picnic.

A large aircraft waited in the center of the meadow. It featured four sets of propeller blades, much like the remote-control drones we played with at home, but much bigger. The main body of the fuselage alone was at least twenty yards long and five yards high.

Soldiers stood guard around the aircraft while crew members entered and exited the vehicle, performing various tasks.

As we approached the aircraft, I looked up at the blades. The sheer size of them confused my depth perception, leaving me dizzy. I lowered my head and took a few deep breaths to prevent nausea.

A shiver went up my spine at the sound of another bellowing grunt. I searched for the source of the sound. From behind the aircraft, a dragon walked forward with a craned neck. It made eye contact with me, sniffed, then raised its head and stood, towering over the aircraft and casting a shadow over it.

One of the soldiers stepped up to the dragon and held out a hand. The dragon lowered its head, allowing him to rub the beast's face.

"Is that a dragon?" I asked, unable to control my surprise.

"Yes, it is, young man," came a voice from behind. I turned back to see Captain Malah hurrying to catch up with me. He was chewing on a stalk of grass he had picked from the meadow. "He's a good friend of mine," he said, pulling out the stalk from his mouth.

"How did you train him?" I asked, trying to sound professional but failing.

"You don't train a dragon," Malah corrected. "You must develop a bond with it."

"Until it gets hungry," the doctor remarked.

I cleared my throat to stifle a laugh that was more disbelief than humor.

A large door opened on the side of the aircraft. We entered and were taken to our seats where Hazi was cuffed to a bracket. Malah loosened my cuffs, then set me next to her.

Two guards approached. *I must be a bigger threat if they have two guards now.* I turned to see Hazi, realizing the guards were more likely for her. My pride deflated.

The craft's interior was spacious. The giant we saw in the forest could easily stand and walk upright in here without hitting his head. I imagined myself tossing a football, playing catch in midflight within the craft's bay area.

Soldiers rushed in and took their seats. Several windows lined the wall next to me. I looked out and saw the dragon step gracefully forward, spread its wings, and flap into the air.

Engines whined. Within seconds the propellers were spinning and lifting us off the ground. I pressed my face closer to the window. Our shift upward was hardly noticeable. Had I not watched the meadow below me shrink into the distance, I would have remained ignorant of our flight. The craft shifted forward, flying over the waterfalls. The aircraft's shadow trailed us on the land below, followed by the shadow of the dragon.

The forest thinned into parks, followed by farmlands and then subdivisions. The residences were replaced by skyscrapers and enormous pyramids. Arenas, or more exactly, colosseums, pockmarked the cityscape.

Hovering vehicles streaked throughout the city. My jaw fell open. I never imagined history being so advanced. It felt like I was watching a futuristic film. But this wasn't the future.

Is this really the past? I asked the doctor, astonished at the world around me.

"Not what you expected, eh?" the doctor whispered.

Our craft flew past the city over what appeared to be a military base. The ground was flat, with cement stretching in every direction.

We stopped our forward motion, hovered, descended, then landed. I turned away from the window, a little disappointed the ride was over. The propellers locked in place, and the soldiers in the craft unbuckled themselves, then exited.

We were escorted out of the craft. Before us were several massive planes resembling the kind I was accustomed to seeing. Seven of them were parked side by side, with a combined wingspan that stretched into the horizon. In the distance, a perimeter of metal fences were topped with what appeared to be razor wires. Green flags fluttered on rock-and-cement buildings.

My hair whipped in the sudden gust of wind from the dragon's wings as it landed on the sunlight-bleached cement nearby.

Captain Malah trotted to the beast, holding out his hand. The dragon, in turn, lowered its head to allow the captain to pat a small area above the large nostrils. The dragon's brow drooped with the captain's touch. They clearly shared a bond.

The dragon blinked, catching sight of me. It scratched its neck with a claw, then lifted its head, maintaining eye contact with me. I felt like a deer staring into the headlights of an oncoming car, unable to move. I'd be an easy snack if the dragon wanted one.

"Hi there," I said, feeling compelled. I gasped when the dragon straightened his head with interest.

Malah double-timed back to us. "I think he likes you," he joked.

The captain pointed to Hazi, then made a quick gesture with his hand. Soldiers, understanding the direction, escorted Hazi away. He then pointed to me, raised his wrists, and spread his arms, signaling the guard to remove my cuffs. I had mixed feelings because I was grateful to be free of the restraints, but I enjoyed the idea of being a threat.

Jet crafts, both large and small, rocketed down runways, shattering all known speed records from my time. "What's your name?" Malah asked, massaging his shoulder.

A jet thundered down a distant runway, so I waited for it to pass before answering. "Keiji," I answered. "My name is Keiji."

"May I call you 'the traveler'?" Malah mused.

"Whatever," I answered, rubbing my wrists. "If that makes you happy."

Malah inhaled sharply. "King Sar is looking forward to meeting you," he said, dropping his hand and hooking his thumbs into his belt.

"I get the impression you know more about me than I do," I concluded.

Malah put his arm around my shoulders and led me away from the aircraft. Our path took us between the large planes ahead, each with a wingspan nearly as wide as a football field. "A few days ago, we picked up a distortion on our radars. The signal wasn't long or strong enough to help us pinpoint a location, so we waited until we picked up another anomaly, and we found it when you entered the forest." Raising his eyebrows, Malah shook his head. "We already had a patrol in the area, so they were able to intercept you quickly."

"You've been looking for me?" I asked.

"Oh yes." Malah leaned his head back. "No doubt, you are from the future." He tapped his lips, referencing the time delay between speaking and understanding.

"I get your interest in me then, and I understand that you arrested the giant for killing a buck, but why arrest her?" I asked, referring to Hazi.

Captain Malah turned to look in Hazi's direction. "She attacked and injured our soldiers." He stopped walking, shrugging his shoulders, about to divulge the real reason for her arrest. "Her people are supposed to inform us in advance before any of them cross into our lands. We received no notice about her."

"What will you do with her?" I asked, trying not to give away my concern for her.

"She will be imprisoned for now," he answered with a soft tone, trying to reassure me. "In the meantime, I will take you to your accommodations."

CHAPTER 6
LATE MORNING

A soldier escorted me to a sparsely lit cement room spacious enough to contain a giant. Hazi sat in the middle, cross-legged and cuffed to a metal eyebolt protruding from the floor. My limbs were free of restraints. "You will remain here," the soldier said, then stepped out of the room.

"What about my accommodations?" I retorted.

"Would you like the cuffs?" he asked, then closed the door, locking it. The guard's footsteps echoed away down the walkway.

"Jackass," I muttered, slapping the door.

"They'll be back for you," Hazi assured, pouting her lip and watching me pace the room. Conscious of the attention, I directed myself behind her and instinctively lifted my arm to smell.

Ugh! I need a shower.

"I could use a bath too," Hazi admitted, as if reading my mind.

I rounded the room, then crossed my legs and plopped down in front of her. "Are you okay?" I asked.

"I'm good. I knew this was going to happen, but it was a little satisfying to get a few licks in on them first. I'll be set free soon enough. Once I prove myself." She grinned.

"What do you have to do to prove yourself?" I asked.

"Defeat a giant in battle in front of a large crowd," she said.

Dumbfounded, I placed an elbow on my knee, then rested my jaw in my hand. "Sounds like a gladiatorial fight to me. Why do you have to fight a giant?"

"You are correct. It is a gladiatorial fight," she said. "I must fight a giant because giants are hated here. Some of my people have been declared enemies of Ganteep because they have befriended giants. To prove I'm not one of them, I must hurt or kill a giant, then I can go free."

"Sounds barbaric," I said, rubbing my temples.

"Of course. Normally this isn't necessary, but the Ganteep government did not know I was coming." She shifted her weight.

"The captain said the same thing."

"Yeah? Well, I wasn't planning on coming to the city until I met you." She stretched her arms. "There's something different about you, and worth the risk of coming here unannounced."

"I am out of place, but it is unnerving that everyone knows it. How can you tell so easily?" I asked.

"You mean apart from the obvious roaming around the wasteland, using wood from failed experiments to build a fire, and your lovely taste in clothes?" she kidded with a sarcastic tone. Her response was rhetorical.

"Failed experiments?" I asked.

"That wood you used to build your fire was from ongoing attempts to make the wasteland soil capable of sustaining plant life. The Ganteep people keep trying to treat the soil and plant trees."

"They clearly made some progress," I admitted. "You said there was a war where you found me?"

"Yes. In fact, the Council of Nine wanted to destroy the humans for it," she muttered under her breath. "The reptilians, though, defended the humans when arguments proceeded about humanity's fate. As it turned out, the reptilians were only interested in a fresh supply of meat."

"Reptilians?" My stomach dropped, and I wanted to puke. To think, humans were to become cows.

"They are a bipedal species who have a particular liking for human meat," she explained.

"Yuck," I said. "Who were the humans fighting?" I asked.

"A faction that wanted humans only for slaves, but King Sar of Ganteep intervened," she said.

"Why did the king help them?" I asked.

"Nobody knows, but there are legends about him befriending a human known as the captain," she said. "Blake, I think, was his name. Their adventures took them to the First Age, where they fought two brothers. Blake killed one, and the other has sworn to avenge his brother's death."

"Who were the two brothers?" I asked, intrigued.

"Multidimensional giants. The older brother, Capriscas, was killed. The younger, Scipio, roamed the earth, then mated with the women, and thus his offspring of giants were born. Scipio made his escape at the battle of the wasteland." She took a deep breath.

"And Blake?" I asked.

"Nobody knows." She grinned. "Now humans fall under the protection of the Council of Nine."

I rose to my feet and outstretched my hand and tapped on the wall. It was solid concrete. "What do you know of dragons?" I asked. "In my time, they are a mere fantasy."

"They are quite rare," she said in a soft tone. "That is the first time I've ever been so close to one, but I have seen them fly before." Hazi tipped her head. "I swear that dragon in the meadow sensed your unique ability in that head of yours."

"Yeah, yeah, yeah," I repeated. "It's of great interest, so I've been told."

Hazi stretched her legs out. "When I talked to you the first time, I sensed no threat, as if you were speaking to me through more than just words."

"My doctor friend says I have an empathic field," I replied, tapping on my temple.

Hazi bit her bottom lip. "That's probably why nobody senses you as a threat," she said, staring at my wrists that were free of cuffs. "Since they left you with me, they are comfortable with us being together, I assume."

I tapped the wall one more time, then returned to a sitting position across from her. "Well then, I'd assume they can sense you too, so why do you have to fight a giant to prove yourself?" I asked, casting a shadow on her theory.

"It's custom, and people like a good fight," she answered.

"Aren't you worried?" I asked, digging my palms into my thighs. "I'd be scared out of my mind."

"I am a hunter of giants, Keiji," she explained in a matter-of-fact tone. "I sell them to people who will take them to places where the giants are free to roam." She contemplated with a smirk. "Honestly, I am more than worried. I'm afraid. Always am."

The voice in my head startled me. "Ask her if she will help you get the scroll," the doctor suggested.

"Is there anything wrong?" Hazi asked.

"No," I answered, pointing to my head. "The doctor wants to know if you'll help me attain the scroll I told you about yesterday."

Hazi threw her head back with a gentle laugh. "It would be a pleasure to help you. What scroll are we in search of?"

What should I tell her?

"Tell her it is a Kantara Scroll," the doctor answered.

I pointed to my head. "The guy up here says it is a Kantara Scroll."

"Hmm." Hazi looked stoic. "If I win this battle, I will be allowed to make a request to Sar, the king of the Ganteep people. Perhaps I can petition for his help to retrieve it."

The door opened, and soldiers filed into the room. One soldier held Hazi's bow and bag of arrows. Another held her spear and ax. A third soldier unfastened Hazi's cuffs and helped her to her feet.

Captain Malah entered the room. "It's time."

CHAPTER 7

Captain Malah finally kept his promise and escorted me to my accommodations where I could clean up. Not just me though. Hazi too.

Hazi and I were taken to a bathhouse. It was a spacious room enclosed with orange-stained glass windows. The walls and floors were made of smoothed bedrock. Aromas of lavender and rosemary filled the air. Candles and incense burned on rock shelves lining the walls. Ceramic pitchers of water with accompanying cups were placed around the room. A bathing pool the size of a tennis court lay before us. Clearly, this was a co-ed bath.

The guards remained outside while young women attended us. They stripped Hazi of her clothes. I tried to avert my eyes, but I thought, *Let's face it, a peek is only natural, right?*

"Right," the doctor answered, reading my thoughts. "I totally agree."

I blushed, knowing that I was not completely alone in my thoughts. "Who could resist gawking at a beautiful woman sharing a bath with me," I whispered.

"I had a wife once, and we met in a bathhouse," the doctor said.

"I really don't care right now," I muttered to the doctor.

The doctor didn't pause. "She took those clothes off, and I was seeing the goods I liked," he said.

"I'm really not interested!" I whispered louder.

"Then she took one look at my goods and winked," the doctor huffed with satisfaction. "Asked her out that very day."

"I can't believe you're telling me this," I muttered.

"Don't be ashamed of your body," the doctor said. "Everyone has one."

"I'm going to drown myself right now," I said, eyeing the water, wanting to stick my head into it and never pull it out again.

The ladies removed my clothes, distracting me from my conversation. My physique was not of a warrior. Between work and school, I had eaten less than I should, drank too much caffeine on a regular basis, and failed to make it to the gym. The result was a body that my friends compared to an anatomy project.

"Oh, I see what you mean," the doctor humored, referring to my body.

"Seriously," I grunted. "We're not going there!"

I tried to act casually despite the embarrassing exchange.

"Are you okay?" asked one of the ladies who was assisting me.

"Just arguing with myself," I answered, not wanting to go into too much detail.

"Well," she said, "I hope you win." She helped me into the warm bath while others took my clothes away for cleaning. Hazi and I each had two naked attendants. The rubbing of their skin against mine suggested the bathhouse likely had many repeat customers.

Embarrassed and uneasy, lopsided smiles were common from me throughout my cleansing. "Do you enjoy this?" I asked the ladies.

"We are designed to," one of them said with a smile.

"Designed?" I asked, confused.

The other girl pressed her finger against my lips. "Just relax," she said, then continued her work.

The girls dried us off, and our clothes were returned. Though my back was toward Hazi, I sneaked several peeks at her. The doctor was abnormally quiet.

Once we were dressed, guards with metal spears entered the bathhouse and escorted us to the king.

***

The doors to the main hall rose at least three times my height. Music from a stringed instrument echoed into my ears as we entered the chamber. At the far end of the room was a wall of windows that looked upon a valley of green fields. In the distance, flying in the air, were four dragons.

Pillars, at least two meters thick, stretched from the floor into a dome-like ceiling, which glowed with a bluish light. The tops of the pillars were decorated with engravings of animal skulls.

The farther we walked, the louder the music grew. We rounded a pillar to see a man playing a lyre-like instrument. Around him, several people occupied couches, each holding a drink. Servants within arm's reach were waiting with glass bottles containing a dark liquid that I assumed to be wine. Guards covered the perimeter.

The musician played a soothing melody, running his fingers across the strings. The crowd swayed with the music. Of all the guests, one figure stuck out as being very different physically, sitting in the center and topping the other guests by at least a head. He wore a headdress that extended backward and had a vaguely bluish tint to his skin. I suspected his skull contained a brain twice the size of mine.

The guests clapped as the music concluded. The musician stood upright, grabbed his instrument, bowed toward the large figure, who nodded in turn, and then took his leave.

The massive figure stood, grinning as he gave me a sideways glance. The guests, all of whom were human, remained seated. The tall figure glided to us, his robe trailing the floor behind. He clasped his hands on my shoulders, bowed his head, then repeated this gesture with Hazi. She returned the nod.

"Welcome to Ganteep City, my friends," he said with a reverberating tone. "I am King Sar." The king's eyes were deep blue. He gestured to a younger man with equally blue eyes, but with blond hair. "This is my son, Prince Sargin."

The prince rose from his seat, then joined his father, taking hold of my hand. Unlike his father, there was nothing alien about him, though Sargin had features that were undeniably like his father's. For example, their jawlines were both sharp, with cleft chins, and their eyes turned upward. "A pleasure," the prince welcomed. On his chest was an emblem of wings, much like the kind airline pilots wore in my day.

"Are you a pilot?" I asked, referring to the wings on his uniform, trying to engage in casual conversation.

"I am," the prince confirmed.

King Sar could not contain himself, clapping his hands together. "When we picked up a time dilation, we hoped for the best. Here you are! The traveler," he winked. Malah's nickname for me had apparently reached the king. "We are very fortunate to have you here, especially with such an incredible gift."

"I assume you are referring to my translation ability," I confirmed.

"I promise you," the doctor interjected, "it isn't for your charming personality!"

With tight lips, I ignored the comment. The doctor's personality was beginning to shine through over the past day.

"He looks a little weak," a guest humored out loud, causing the other guests on the couch to laugh.

King Sar gently waved a hand. In response, they reduced their laughter to mere chuckles. "You have to forgive them, Keiji," Sar said apologetically. The king returned to his seat. A servant handed him a glass of wine, and he took a sip.

Prince Sargin stepped forward to Hazi, who in turn lowered her head. Sargin did the same. "You'd be welcomed with wide arms if we knew of your visit," he stated, squinting with confusion.

"I understand the risk I took," she assured.

"I'm looking forward to the event," the prince admitted. "Nobody has seen a gladiatorial spectacle in quite some time. There is quite a bit of excitement in the city." The prince gave a half grin.

Pictures of gladiators hacking at each other with J-shaped swords and blocking each thrust with a curved shield sped like a carousel through my mind. "You are not what I picture when I think of gladiators," I admitted to Hazi. "Do you fight to the death?"

"Not usually. An opponent can submit by extending an index finger," Hazi said. "If an opponent refuses to submit, then unconsciousness or death are the only options."

Sargin stepped in. "Death is never the goal, per se, but it is a risk," he admitted. "Beating to submission is good enough."

"Does the giant know that?" I asked rhetorically. I turned to Hazi with a quick idea. "Don't fight. Just surrender," I suggested with worry for her safety.

Hazi propped her hands on her hips. "Impossible," she said. "A giant does not accept submission, and they will not surrender except for one reason."

"What's the reason?" I urged.

King Sar and all his guests leaned in to hear. "If I told you, these guys would rig the fight against me," she answered, jabbing her thumb back toward the king.

King Sar threw his head back in laughter. "That we would," he admitted with pride.

Hazi dropped her hands and rubbed them together. "Besides, I need to win to have my request granted."

Prince Sargin opened his mouth to speak, but snapped it shut. With a grin, he clapped his hands. "Fantastic!" he exclaimed, "Your people never disappoint. May you be victorious, and your request granted."

I was distracted by the sun flickering through the windows. I glanced out in search of the cause. My investigation was short-lived, as two dragons chased each other in a sort of tag-like game in the sky.

"Beautiful, aren't they," King Sar said, standing up again and stepping to my side. I nodded with agreement. The king put his arm around my shoulder and led me to the window. "If you ever stare at a dragon in the eyes, you will understand that he is intelligent, calculating, and most importantly, is very aware of you staring back at him." Sar patted my shoulder. "Come to think of it. You may be the first person to someday get into the head of one."

One of the dragons nose-dived, and the other followed, spraying a long, powerful streak of fire. At the bottom of the valley lay the dragon I met before, watching the spectacle above but evidently tired of the chaos. He leaped into the air, dwarfing the other dragons with his sheer size. He roared at them, spraying a stream of white-hot fire. The two dragons dropped to the ground and curled up, succumbing to the largest of the bunch.

"That's Enkidu," Sar pointed out. "He's the alpha."

"Enkidu," I repeated. "He's awesome." Enkidu's coat of scales glittered in the sunlight.

"That he is, Keiji," Sar agreed.

"Your highness," a man said. "Do you have a moment?"

A uniformed man approached the king, accompanied by soldiers. His outfit was more rugged than Captain Malah's uniform, but based on what I could tell of his insignia, he was a person of great rank.

"Yes, General Laroche," the king said. "What do you need?"

"I have an update for you about the object approaching the planet," the general informed the king while surveying the occupants nearby.

"What object?" I asked.

The general ignored my question. He stood about six feet tall and was imposing in both his muscular frame and his scarred face. The king stepped away to speak with the general in private.

"Doesn't look like good news," Prince Sargin whispered to Captain Malah. Malah remained still, giving nothing away.

The king and the general exchanged a few muffled words. The general bowed and exited with his accompanying soldiers following. King Sar returned to us, frowning.

"What happened, Father?" the anxious prince asked.

King Sar waved Sargin to be silent, then turned to Hazi. "Everything is set. Are you ready?"

Hazi squinted. "As ready as I'll ever be. Take me to the challenger."

Chapter 8
MIDDAY

The king invited me to join him at the colosseum. Outside, I heard an announcer speak gibberish through an intercom. I concentrated, attempting to decipher what was being said. *Why do I not understand what the announcer is saying?*

Reading my thoughts, the doctor answered. "You're out of proximity to the announcer, so you are just hearing words. Be patient. The translation will come soon," the doctor reassured.

A set of doors opened to a balcony overlooking a magnificent stadium filled with people who cheered when the king entered. "Sit next to me," he ordered, lowering himself into the middle seat. I complied, taking the seat to his immediate left. Sargin took the seat on the king's right, and Captain Malah took a post, standing behind the group. Women entered the suite and sat down in seats behind us, and guards maintained their positions at the entrance.

People in the stands were milling about while attendants moved up and down the stairwells offering merchandise, snacks, and beverages. Ushers escorted guests to their seats. Balconies and private boxes lined the stadium, where elite observers looked on, many of whom were smoking. The place smelled of perfumes, tobacco, alcohol, and dust.

In the arena below, dancers entertained the audience to slow-tempo instrumental music. The dance was reminiscent of ballet. As the tempo sped up, the dancers kept the pace. The dance became sultry as the entertainers pressed their bodies against each other. They fell to the ground when a shot fired with a loud crack.

Percussion instruments pounded at a faster pace. The dancers transformed into acrobats, throwing each other into the air with nimbleness and agility. Each was clothed in dark, tightly fitted leather and had white stripes smeared across their face.

While the king focused on the show, I had a chance to study him free of any disruptions. He was human-like, but not quite. Sitting this close, the wrinkles in his skin suggested he had lived to an incredible age.

"How old are you?" I asked without thinking.

"Old," he answered, never diverting his attention from the dancers below.

Torches fired in the hands of the dancers, who then swung their arms, making incredible art of flames into thin air. Two men threw spears from across the arena to each other with elegance. Each caught the other's spear and sent them flying straight up. The spears hit the ground, and sudden silence and darkness fell. The dancers sped out from the arena.

Lights beamed at our box and onto King Sar, who promptly jumped to his feet and stood before a microphone.

"For all to see and all to know, I present you with a hunter whose fate is to be determined," King Sar proclaimed. "She claims to be a friend. Today's contender is Hazi!"

The colosseum erupted in cheer as Hazi stepped onto the field with her bow, spear, and ax. A guard ceremonially hurled a spear that stuck upright in the center of the arena, and Hazi took her place next to it. I focused my attention on her and felt anxiety that mounted to fear. I wasn't sure if it was mine or hers that I sensed. I glanced around feeling nothing, but each time I focused my attention on her, the feelings returned.

"And her opponent," King Sar continued, "the filth of creation. The image of violence and inappropriate relations between those above and the women below. The epitome of all that is horrid in this world. He has a name that will be lost to us all, but tonight, his name will join the many others that will suffer defamation, even death." Sar paused and turned to his right, the opposite of Hazi. "The name is Baugi," he announced, in a slow, low voice that sent shivers up my spine.

A monstrous giant entered the arena wielding a spear in one hand and a shield in the other. It was the same giant we saw in the forest. He curled his lips, scowling at the booing crowd as he approached the ceremonial spear that mirrored Hazi's. Baugi dropped his shield, shoved his spear into the ground, and then tied his long hair into a bun, readying himself for battle. With his hair out of his face, he inspected the ceremonial spear, and without warning grasped it and hurled it at Hazi, but she twisted out of the way.

"Oh crap!" the king hollered. "The fight has begun!"

Baugi grunted, evaluating his opponent, and grasped the spear he entered the arena with.

Hazi pulled out her bow and rapidly fired arrows at Baugi. The giant, being of greater mass, was not able to move as quickly. He used his shield to repel the arrows, but one struck him in the shin. He hollered and dropped to the other knee. With his shield, he snapped the arrow in half leaving the head still in his shin.

Hazi returned her bow to her back. She gripped both her ax and spear, trotting to Baugi.

Baugi hoisted himself up to his feet and readied his spear for battle. I gripped the arms of my chair, fearing that Baugi would crush Hazi with his sheer mass. Hazi danced around the giant just outside of his strike zone. He lunged at her several times but missed. He was tiring quickly.

Hazi watched her opponent without blinking. Baugi, though, began to blink incessantly from the sweat dripping off his face. He lunged at her with his spear and missed. Out of frustration, he threw his shield at her and tried to follow with a spear strike. But Hazi moved in quickly, parried the giant's spear with her ax, and jabbed her own spear into Baugi's left eye. He howled and pulled at the spear, ripping it out and leaving behind an empty, bloody socket.

I cringed at the sight.

Baugi threw the spear to the ground where Hazi stood. She stepped forward, leaving the bloodied spear behind, not fazed by the scene in front of her. She pulled out her bow and loaded an arrow. Baugi lifted his head to face her, and she took aim at his other eye.

Baugi lowered his head and put both hands onto the ground, cowering down.

"Submit!" Hazi commanded, hands steady while keeping the arrow firmly locked in place.

Baugi only moaned, clearly not a threat, but Hazi continued to yell at him.

"He's done!" I announced to the king.

"He has to surrender," the king said nonchalantly, holding up his index finger, "or the fight must continue."

I turned to Baugi, closed my eyes, and concentrated all my thoughts on him, picturing closed fists and an extended index finger pointing to the king.

The crowd erupted in cheers. I opened my eyes to see Baugi doing exactly as I pictured, but the king's attention was on me, studying my undertaking with amusement.

My heart skipped a beat with excitement for Baugi but sank in disappointment when guards fired on him with stun blasters, knocking the giant unconscious. The crowd cheered again as Hazi raised her bow in victory.

King Sar stood up, along with the rest of the people in the balcony, and clapped at the victory. "I'm not sure what impresses me most," the king admitted. "Her defeating the giant or you getting him to extend his finger." He winked at me.

Two soldiers fixed metallic devices onto the giant. One pulled out a remote-control device and floated the giant into midair. With this antigravity technology, they easily pushed him away.

Hazi faced the king and bowed.

King Sar lifted his hands, silencing the crowd. "Mighty Hazi, you represent your people well, and we gladly welcome you to Ganteep City as a friend," he decreed for all to hear. "Your giant has submitted, and his injury will serve as a warning to other giants who want to trample on our land. We are indebted to you."

The crowd chanted her name. Hazi smiled, enjoying all the attention. I looked back to see Malah nodding with approval, but the women behind him remained seated, chins up with restrained discipline, keeping their composure for the dignity of the king but snubbing their noses at Hazi. I wondered if any of the women in the king's entourage were the prince's mother, but none of them displayed any motherly affection or wifely subjection to the king.

King Sar sat back down, allowing his son to stand in front of the crowd. Sargin waved his arm, silencing the arena. "Great warrior," he began, "you have defeated a giant, and it is customary for the king to grant you one request."

Hazi stepped forward. "If it pleases the king, I'd prefer to ask in private."

The king tilted his head toward me, suspecting I had some foreknowledge. I ignored him. The king nodded to the prince, agreeing to her request.

"Of course. Come," the prince invited her, waving his hand inward.

The crowd booed with the unexpected privacy of the request, then began exiting. Their noise faded as Hazi was brought to the balcony.

The king clasped her shoulders with his hands, bowed his head with appreciation, and then waved his pointer finger. "The eye, eh?"

"Yes," Hazi admitted. One of the ladies in the back approached Hazi, inspected her wrist, wrapped it, and returned to her position behind the king. Hazi clenched her fist with satisfaction. "Giants fear losing their sight more than death. If I took out an eye, he'd succumb to protect the other one."

"Fascinating," the king said. "Just as fascinating as watching the traveler use his mind to teach the giant how to submit with his pointer. I assume your request requires some discretion."

"Yes, your highness," she answered. "The request originates with Keiji."

"The traveler," Malah interjected. "Seems fitting."

"Ah," the king answered, then raised his eyebrows and returned his attention back to Hazi. "Go ahead then," he insisted.

"Keiji needs to attain a Kantara Scroll," she stated with bluntness.

The king clasped his hands together with an exaggerated sigh. "I am very grateful for your discretion, mighty Hazi," he said, acutely aware of what the request meant.

"I will retract my petition if it is inappropriate," Hazi said, sensing the potential issue with the request.

King Sar shook his head. "No. You have earned the right to solicit anything you want, short of any position in my house or government," the king humored. "The scroll is not here, but I know where it is." King Sar took a deep breath. "It's in Midlatica, at the center of the planet."

CHAPTER 9
A LITTLE PAST MIDDAY

King Sar led us outside the colosseum to a courtyard hosting tall statues of human figures. He regaled us with stories about some of the figures he knew from a time long beyond imagining. He stopped at a massive boulder that had not yet been sculpted. "This will be my son," the king announced. "When he takes over, they will sculpt his likeness."

Prince Sargin smiled and bowed. "I am honored, Father."

Sounds of boots clapping down on concrete grew louder. We turned to see General Laroche walking toward us. "We have received a message from Admiral Radau."

The king steepled his fingers together and took a deep breath. The general escorted us out of the courtyard into an underground facility that housed hundreds of military personnel. After passing through several security stations, we entered a war room where display screens were stacked at least three stories high. The screens displayed military grids and trajectories.

A soldier approached the general and whispered an update. General Laroche turned around. "Admiral Radau is on the comm."

King Sar placed one hand on his hip and gestured with his other hand to patch the admiral through.

Admiral Radau's voice reverberated into the room from the intercom, but I heard only gibberish since the language was transmitted through a device only. Radau paused, then spoke again, and the room erupted with frenzied conversations. The king ordered silence in the room so he could hear Radau.

Hazi, sensing my dilemma, translated in a whisper. "There is a large object, about a sixth the size of our planet, approaching rapidly. Scans indicate the object is causing tidal disruptions in our oceans."

The next words I heard from Admiral Radau were translated. "We believe the planet's surface will be flooded," the admiral speculated. "The magnetic poles of the planet are already shifting."

I shot a glance back at Hazi in shock. "Your translator is working then," she observed, tapping her temple.

I nodded in answer. "The voice is staticky, but I can understand." I assumed Hazi, when she translated for me, somehow Rosetta-stoned the language Radau was speaking for my translator.

A mumbling could be heard from the loudspeaker, and then Radau said, "Reconnaissance."

Laroche stepped to the intercom. "Proceed with the reconnaissance probe," the general ordered in agreement with the admiral's apparent recommendation.

The center screen flicked and projected a view from the probe. Other screens showed live shots of the admiral's ship that resembled a floating city. "That ship is monstrous," I said out loud.

"It's a battlecarrier," Malah explained, "capable of holding hundreds of fighters and thousands of soldiers. There are three of them up there. Radau's ship is called *Nemesis*."

The center screen flashed to show the probe exiting the *Nemesis* and streaking toward the object. It scanned the surface and transmitted data to our viewing screens. I was unable to read any of the verbiage.

Admiral Radau piped up. "My science officer here is convinced that the object is the egg of a space dragon."

The people in the war room broke out in muffled conversation. King Sar raised his eyebrows. "Space dragons were assumed to be mythical creatures," he said, tapping his fingers on a nearby console.

"What if there is a dragon in there?" The general wondered.

"According to the scans, the egg is hollow," the admiral conveyed over the intercom. "Somehow, the dragon has been extracted without breaking the shell."

"Guys," I interjected. "That's the moon!"

King Sar raised an eyebrow but said nothing.

I rolled my head, staring at the king. "I mean, it looks like the moon. Much smoother than the one in my time though." I felt like cowering under his disparaging looks.

"There is no moon orbiting this planet," Sar said. "Never has been." The king returned his attention to the commotion in the room.

"Well, in my time, there is," I muttered.

"I know," Sar said unexpectedly. "Blake used to describe it to me," he muttered.

"What?" I was surprised.

"Who is that, and what language is he speaking?" Radau asked, hearing my voice over the speakers. Before he could receive an answer, the admiral redirected his attention. "Hold on. We are picking up an energy source."

The probe screen flashed and turned to snow.

"We lost our feed to the probe," General Laroche informed the admiral.

The admiral did not answer right away. "We are switching to visual scanners. Nothing. Nothing. Wait!" the admiral exclaimed. "We have debris. It appears our probe was destroyed. Our scanners have picked up residuals consistent with the use of a pulse cannon."

"What does that mean?" I asked.

"It was shot down," Malah answered.

"General," called out a communications officer at one of the workstations, "Our other two battlecarriers, the *Berlitz* and the *Friedman*, have arrived and joined the *Nemesis*," he said, then pressed a transmitter lodged in his ear, listening. "The admiral has officially acknowledged command."

"Sir," another officer called. "The object is accelerating toward us."

Radau piped in over the intercom. "That is confirmed. The object is speeding up."

King Sar bit his lip. "What is your recommendation?" he asked, trusting the admiral, who had direct eyes on the situation.

"Destroy it before it reaches the planet," the admiral answered.

The king nodded his head. I wanted to reach out to the doctor, but my thoughts were scrambled. I could only watch, trying to keep up with something in the present that was technically part of my past. This did not feel like the past.

General Laroche picked up the microphone. "Admiral Radau, you have permission to engage."

CHAPTER 10
EARLY AFTERNOON

The three battlecarriers veered off from each other to take orbit in equidistant positions around the moon. Their firing commenced immediately at the surface. Within minutes, dust clouds covered the object.

"We are not penetrating the surface," the admiral informed us. "That shell has been reinforced. Hold on."

Red lights blinked in the war room. An explosion was heard on the intercom.

"Admiral," the general called, "report."

"The object just fired a missile," the admiral said. "We are climbing altitude to keep our distance."

Alarms whirred; trajectories blinked; commotion stirred.

"Sir," a woman's voice yelled from below. "Hyperspace windows are opening. Lots of them!"

Hyperspace windows? I wondered.

The doctor broke his silence. "Hyperspace is a higher dimension in which ships can travel faster than the speed of light," he informed me. "If a hyperspace window is opening, then something's about to arrive."

"We are tracking over a hundred hyperspace windows opening," the admiral confirmed, "and several hundred reptilian warcruisers just appeared on our radars."

"Reptilians!" Sargin cried. "It's a trap!"

The Ganteep battlecarriers regrouped to meet the newcomers head on.

Red blips depicting the enemy covered the viewscreens in the war room. Three blue blips depicted the *Nemesis*, the *Berlitz*, and the *Friedman*. Dashes crossed between the red and blue blips. I didn't need to guess what the dashes represented. The two fleets were firing on each other.

Sargin turned to his father. "We have to do something!"

"There is nothing we can do to help," King Sar said. "The admiral knows what to do."

"Then I'll do something," Sargin announced. He rounded on General Laroche. "Get ready to defend ourselves against a surface attack!"

General Laroche bit the inside of his cheeks, thinking about the implications of the order, then glanced at the king. Sar tucked his chin, deflating his chest in defeat with no other alternatives to offer. Laroche hung up the microphone, bowed, then rushed out of the room.

I watched the battle play out on-screen. The *Nemesis* and the *Berlitz* flanked a reptilian ship and wreaked havoc with cannon fire. The reptilian vessel exploded while Radau's engaged an enemy on the opposite side. A moment later, the *Nemesis* struck an enemy ship with a cannon, causing it to veer off its vector, hosting a series of explosions until the ship disintegrated.

The *Friedman* positioned itself above the *Nemesis* and the *Berlitz*, providing coverage fire.

A new set of alarms blared as the room flashed red.

Malah stepped forward. "Your Highness, we must leave."

King Sar turned back. "I will not tuck tail and run, Captain," the king stated with eyes blazing.

Captain Malah stepped back and nodded.

"The enemy is launching fighters," the admiral announced. "We have already launched ours!"

Within seconds, multiple viewing screens across the walls were filled with videos from cockpit cameras. The reptilians swarmed the Ganteep fleet and overwhelmed them. I watched a fighter blast three reptilian vessels into debris before the screen went blank and switched to another camera.

Admiral Radau turned the *Nemesis* hard to port, exposing the side of his battlecarrier, and barraged the enemy fighters with all sorts of weaponry. With missiles, Radau destroyed several enemy warcruisers.

Various viewscreens stopped their signals, while another screen brightened with the explosion of the battlecarrier, the *Berlitz*, disintegrating before our eyes.

The room stood silent, watching the horrific scene. My breath escaped me as the image of thousands of lives lost burned itself into my brain.

Radau's ship kept its fire on the attacking fleet while the *Friedman* pushed forward, firing everything it had. A dozen reptilian warcruisers dropped off the radar at a rapid pace with each major eruption of fire from the Ganteep battlecarrier, but it was being choked out by the storm of the overwhelming enemy. The reptilians flanked the *Friedman*, and despite a valiant effort, it suffered the fate of its sister ship, the *Berlitz*.

With two battlecarriers down, the reptilian fleet split, with one group maintaining its attack on Radau while the others headed to the planet's surface.

My attention was tethered to the lower left screen where one of the Ganteep fighters took command of a squadron, flying in a V-formation. They took a position behind a large reptilian ship. The fighters on the flanks plowed a path for the inner fighters to fly close to the warcruiser ahead and launch missiles into the reptilian ship's thrusters, which started a cascade of explosions that disintegrated the ship into a million pieces.

The fighters pushed forward, seeking a second target. They achieved the same success with another warcruiser, but the reptilian fighters caught on to the strategy and, with blunt force, rammed into the Ganteep fighters, destroying them along with themselves.

Sargin, who watched the scene unfold with me, refused to blink. "They are desperate if they are ramming their own ships into ours."

Admiral Radau's voice piped in through the intercom. "We cannot win, but we will fight until we can fight no more," he said. A loud explosion overwhelmed the intercom.

The king grabbed the microphone. "Admiral," he said, "may the courage and honor of you and your fleet be remembered for all time."

The *Nemesis* plunged itself into the heart of the reptilian attackers, discharging every weapon available as enemy craft swarmed around it. Radau's defending vessels were thinned to the point of nonexistence.

"We have nothing left to fire," the admiral informed us.

Nearly two dozen large reptilian vessels closed in on Radau's ship. Radau rammed his vessel into the foremost attacker, tearing it in half.

"One thing left to do," Radau announced.

One of the satellites orbiting the battle focused its camera on the admiral's ship, which displayed on the only monitor left showing a live feed. My heart stopped as the *Nemesis* exploded, destroying all enemy ships within a large radius. It was clear that a nuclear weapon had been detonated.

The king closed his eyes, mourning.

Sargin took a deep breath. "The Council of Nine will punish us for using that weapon," he warned his father.

"It had to be done," the king insisted, opening his eyes. "Does it matter what the council thinks now?"

The remaining reptilian ships regrouped and navigated to our planet with nothing in their way. The dragon egg was left behind them. I never imagined that the pocked face of our moon was partially the result of a large space battle.

King Sar rested a hand on my shoulder, then laid the other on his son's shoulder. "Young Prince," the king called to his son without moving his posture. "I want you and Malah to take the traveler and Hazi to Midlatica and retrieve the Kantara Scroll."

Malah stepped forward. "I will remain by your side," he said, making it clear he intended to stay with his king.

King Sar dropped his arms. "You are my most trusted guard, and I want you to protect my son to the best of your ability," he said, refusing Malah's offer. "I must stay at the capitol building. If I fall, my son will need you, so you will go with the prince."

Malah, without fidgeting, bowed. "It will be as you order."

Sar pulled me to the side so that we were alone. "Your path will cross that of an old friend of mine, Captain Elton Blake," he said in perfect English with a voice so low only I could hear. "When you see him, tell him not to take the grant. All he needs is endurance."

"What?" I asked with a whisper, shocked. "Don't take the grant? All he needs is endurance?" I confirmed.

"You heard me correctly," the king said, then turned to rest his eyes on his son one last time. "Go," he urged in his native language. "There isn't much time!"

PART II

CHAPTER 11
AFTERNOON

Sirens blasted, alerting the Ganteep citizens of an imminent attack. Swarms of people panicked, racing to find protection. Soldiers pushed their way through crowds, clearing a path for my companions and me to follow.

"We must get to the airfield," Malah informed our escorts.

A soldier acknowledged the order and took us to an opening covered by a reddish laser-like blanket. The troops ran through this force field.

"Malah, help them," Sargin ordered.

Malah extended his arm, holding up his hands for Hazi and me to stop. "One second," he said, adjusting a device on his wrist, then grabbed both of us by the shoulders. My skin felt hypersensitive with Malah's touch. "Go!" Malah ordered, and he pushed us forward. Every muscle in my body twitched when we passed through the field.

"That felt crazy," I said out loud, feeling my skin return to normal when the captain let us go.

Malah lifted his sleeve, giving us a better view of a bracelet. "This allows us to pass through barriers such as this," Malah explained, pointing at the one we just passed through.

Screaming erupted from behind, and I turned to witness the commotion of desperate civilians fleeing for their lives, attempting to enter through the portal. The force field surged with electricity, setting them on fire. They fell to the ground, convulsing, as their bodies burned to a blackened heap. I started to breathe faster, feeling the adrenaline rush heightening my flight instincts with the sudden reality of mortal danger.

We dashed past several heaps of metallic spare parts and entered a spacious hangar bay where we caught up with Sargin and the other soldiers. Floating skiffs with open tops were parked in a row, each capable of holding a dozen occupants. Cannons and machine guns were hoisted on top. Yellow lights emitted a soft glow beneath a skiff that soldiers were boarding.

Soldiers prepped the vehicle for launch and loaded the machine guns with ammunition belts and charged their own pistols. Sargin took a position at the helm. Hazi leaped on with ease, then reached down with both arms and pulled me on board. Malah entered the craft using a set of mobile stairs on the opposite side.

A broad door opened ahead, also protected by the same reddish force field we passed through earlier. The skiff was thrust forward. We gripped the railings on the side to maintain our balance.

Malah wrapped his arm around Hazi and me right before we approached the field. Once through, Malah let go. This time, I felt only the tickling of butterflies in my stomach.

We raced through the city with wind whipping through our hair. I gripped the railing with both hands to prevent myself from falling over as we swerved to avoid colliding with buildings, obelisks, and other structures.

Directly ahead, a pyramid-shaped skyscraper stood alone like a beacon of freedom, then it disappeared, engulfed in an enormous explosion, hit by a weapon from the sky. I buried my head into my chest, protecting my eyes from the brightness. Once the sound of the explosion settled, I looked up to see the sky filled with large spacecrafts firing at the surface. A barrage of explosions erupted all around and throughout the cityscape.

Reptilian vessels descended on the city and bombarded the deflection field around the capitol building at the center of Ganteep City where Sar remained. Defenders manned anti-aircraft cannons, punishing the enemy. Reptilian aggressors crashed into the building and streets, cascading in a blanket of flames. The reptilians destroyed the protective cannons. The king's only protection was the force field, and it just collapsed.

The attacking vessels switched to missile fire, and white streaks descended on the centermost building, causing a brilliant eruption that resembled a star going supernova. I was knocked to the floor when the shock wave swept over us.

My heart felt heavy, knowing that the king was most assuredly dead. I whipped my head around to Sargin, but his attention was focused on flying the skiff. If he knew what happened to his father, he was keeping it to himself.

We heard a buzzing from above. I searched for the source of the sound but found nothing at first. Then the sound grew louder as several small crafts resembling bodysuits with guns descended on the city.

One of the soldiers recognized the small crafts. "Infiltrators!" he yelled.

"Keep them off us," Malah ordered.

The infiltrators swooped down, blowing up several buildings. In a desperate attempt to protect themselves, people fell to the ground. The infiltrators swarmed like bees with a vengeance, setting the people on fire and riddling their bodies with bullets.

A blast shook our skiff, and a soldier was knocked overboard. I looked up to see several infiltrators chasing us. "We have company!" I yelled.

"You think?" Sargin yelled back with sarcasm, accelerating the skiff to full throttle.

Soldiers on the skiff took aim at the attacking vessels and fired, but the infiltrators shot back, striking one soldier in the face. Hazi grabbed her bow and fired an onslaught of arrows at the enemy, but her arrows bounced off the infiltrators' armor. She jumped behind a cannon and pulled the trigger, hitting an infiltrator, sending it to the streets below like a meteorite.

Enemy transporters landed and disgorged armored reptilian troopers using ramps. Ganteep servicemen engaged the enemy, trying to hold them at bay, but most were mowed down by reptilian strafing attacks. Civilians attempting to flee were caught in the crossfire between the fighting factions.

We reached the outskirts of the city where the land flattened. Sargin accelerated.

Hazi's weapon jammed. She slapped the gun, but with no effect. One of the soldiers helped Hazi open the cover assembly, dislodge a shell, and slapped it shut. An infiltrator's weapon blew a hole in the soldier's chest. Hazi took aim and fired, avenging the soldier's death and sending the infiltrator spiraling to the ground amidst punishing flames.

Malah directed fire to an approaching vessel. I picked up a weapon from a fallen soldier and joined Malah, following his directions. Having shot many rifles in my own time, this weapon felt natural. I pulled the trigger at a steady pace, remembering the lessons my father taught to stay calm and collected.

The floor rocked when an infiltrator landed on the skiff. Its thrusters transformed into legs, with rotating guns on the side. The infiltrator's cockpit was now upright, and in a window above, I could make out the shape of its occupant.

The infiltrator shot down three soldiers with one blast, then took aim at our cockpit. Hazi abandoned the cannon and thrust her spear into the vessel's window, piercing the occupant's head. Hazi jerked the spear out, and Sargin spun the skiff to the port side, throwing the infiltrator overboard.

"What the hell is in that thing?" I asked, stunned at how easy the archaic-looking spearhead could crush through the windshield and kill the driver.

"I'll tell you later," she said, running back to the cannon.

The remaining infiltrators regrouped and chased us, but they were soon caught up in explosions as cannon fire streaked above. I

KANTARA | THE TRAVELER   75

turned to see our airfield ahead, wrapped by a force field. Cannons on the airfield's perimeter blasted cover fire.

Malah grabbed Hazi around the waist, but simply grasped my forearm.

"What the hell is this?" I murmured, noticing how closely Malah held Hazi to his body.

"Focus," the doctor urged, bringing me back to the reality that we had an enemy trying to kill us.

The skiff swooped in through the force field and came to a stop on a tarmac. I looked around us. The only ones left of our party were Hazi, Malah, Sargin, three soldiers, and me.

It was the first time I had ever fought in a battle.

CHAPTER 12

LATER IN THE AFTERNOON

The force field protecting the airfield thumped from the barrage of the enemy's assault. Reptilian motherships and smaller warcruisers positioned themselves to crush the defensive weapons on the airfield's perimeter. Troops disembarked from reptilian transports and hastily assembled cannons.

Ganteep pilots scrambled their fighters to defend the airfield. The reptilian ships were smaller with more maneuverability, but the Ganteep fighters pounded them with superior firepower, precision missiles, and better training in dogfighting. A Ganteep fighter destroyed the enemy's cannon arsenal using strafing runs.

Three fighter jets raced across the perimeter and fired, decimating several reptilian crafts with ease, but then were taken by surprise when one of the reptilian motherships launched missiles. Above, as if by instinct, a fighter launched a missile of its own before its wing was clipped, causing it to spin out of control. The stray missile locked onto an infiltrator, destroying it.

Several larger Ganteep aircrafts flew in from another airfield and sped toward the enemy. The fighter jets took flanking positions to provide cover fire while the larger aircraft took aim, hitting several weak points in a warcruiser, erupting it into a blaze of fire.

Reptilian warcruisers launched fighter crafts of their own and overwhelmed the Ganteep fighters by their superior numbers.

Below the raging battle, under the safeguard of the force field, we exited the skiff, joined on the ground by an airman. "We got the message, and your plane is ready," he said.

Captain Malah thanked the airman, who remained by his side.

"That shield will not hold up for long," Sargin warned.

Captain Malah surveyed the skiff that brought us to safety. Two soldiers lay dead in the middle, horribly mutilated. He removed bracelets off each, then gave one to Hazi and one to me. "Put those on," he requested. Once they were affixed to our wrists, Malah tapped them with his own bracelet. My bracelet activated and wrapped itself snugly, but comfortably, around my wrist. "You won't have any problems with Ganteep force fields now."

Sargin rubbed his hands together with anticipation. "Let's go," he insisted.

The airman led the way off the tarmac to the airfield. Thudding above reverberated in our eardrums. We ran toward the only stationary plane. Though we were sprinting, the veritable size of the winged vehicle made it feel like we were standing still.

Hazi was the first to reach the craft. Once we were all on board, Hazi jumped in and secured the door with the help of the airman, who remained outside.

The inside of the vessel was sizable but practically empty. "This is big enough to rescue hundreds of people," I said, insinuating that we should use this flying machine to help victims flee.

"Not now, Keiji," Malah screamed back. "That is not our mission."

"Up here," Sargin yelled.

We raced up the staircase and stepped into a large cockpit. A pilot sat in a bucket seat, punching buttons in preparation for takeoff. Sargin slipped into the copilot's seat. He buckled himself in, then flipped toggle switches on the instrument panel. The engines roared to life.

"Find a place to sit," Sargin urged. We ran through a narrow corridor to the carpeted passenger cabin, still close to the cockpit where we could hear Sargin speak to the pilot. All seats were placed with their backs to the front.

Hazi sat at the rear of the aircraft, giving her plenty of legroom. I hopped into the seat closest to the exit and strapped in, with Malah opposite me.

The plane shook with the sound of an explosion. My body lurched forward. I glanced out the window to see that we were moving. The plane vibrated again with another explosion.

"They have broken through," Malah yelled through the corridor into the cockpit, making it known that the force field had collapsed.

Sargin yelled back. "I know!"

Our plane accelerated.

"We're not going to make it," Hazi shouted, leaning over to the window in her row.

"Yes, we will!" Sargin yelled back.

Infiltrators swarmed and fired at our craft.

"Does this thing have any defensive weapons?" Hazi asked Malah.

"No," he hollered.

"Be quiet!" Sargin insisted.

"They're getting closer," I said, watching an infiltrator race so closely that I could see the scaly face of the reptilian within.

The plane taxied to the runway and promptly began accelerating to take-off speed.

"We're not going to make it," Sargin yelled to the pilot as blasts from the infiltrators shook the aircraft.

Hazi shouted back. "I thought you said we were going to make it!"

"I'm not talking to you," Sargin shot back.

I cuffed my ears, feeling helpless. The plane rattled when a bright light flashed in my window. I feared we had exploded, but the engines were still roaring, and our acceleration continued.

My body flushed with warmth, sensing a strong presence nearby. Through the window I watched Enkidu, the dragon, grasp an infiltrator with his claw and hurl it to the ground, smashing it to pieces. He launched fire from his mouth, and reptilians evaporated in the flames. Three other dragons wreaked havoc on other attackers. Everyone aboard watched the dragons make quick work of the enemy. We cheered for the brave animals, but our cheer was short-lived.

I doubled over in pain to a sudden screech that pounded in my head. Instinctively, I turned to the window and watched one of the dragons fall to the ground, hit by fire from a reptilian warcruiser. I glanced around the cabin to see if anybody else heard it, but they appeared oblivious to the sound. Their attention was solely focused on the events unfolding outside. My skin shivered with the realization that I was hearing a dragon cry out in pain before his demise.

The remaining dragons kept fighting, protecting us as the plane raced down the runway.

"What's going on?" the doctor asked.

A dragon was just killed, I answered.

"We can't lose them," the doctor warned.

What the hell can I do about that? I asked angrily.

A second dragon hit the ground with a barrel roll, and the scream in my head nearly split my skull. Inadvertently, I flung myself to the back of the seat, gripping my ears until the pain subsided, then returned my attention to the events unfolding outside.

The third dragon crushed infiltrators and spewed fire, but it was struck in the back and plummeted into the runway. I heard wailing in my head, filled with grief.

Enkidu, the only dragon left, fought on with intense aggression. He used claws, fire breath, teeth, wings, and chest as weapons to defend us.

Our aircraft lifted off the ground. Climbing, we gained speed. Enkidu followed us, providing protection. Soon, our aircraft outpaced the attacking infiltrators. The sounds of battle ceased, and all that could be heard was the hum of engines.

"Is everyone okay?" Sargin asked.

Malah unbuckled himself and headed toward the cockpit. "All good, it seems."

I unbuckled and joined Malah.

"We are losing fuel fast," Sargin informed us, pointing to a light on the dashboard.

"How far can we go?" Malah asked.

"According to these sensors, there is a downed craft ahead in the Land of Darmant. It's probably the same one that was taking Hazi's friend back to his homeland," Sargin speculated.

"Hazi's friend?" I asked.

"The giant she fought just a few hours ago, Baugi," Sargin said. "That craft may have what we need. If we can get there, we should be able to find some transports inside that can get us to Outpost One, a Ganteep stronghold."

"But?" I asked, sensing there was more to the story.

"We don't have enough fuel to get that far, so we'll have to journey by foot in the Land of Darmant if we are going to make it there. The Land of Darmant is a stomping ground for giants," Sargin warned.

I whirled back to where Hazi sat. "I guess we are lucky to have a giant hunter then," I admitted.

Malah nodded in agreement.

"How do we land?" I asked, now concerned with the more immediate obstacle.

"There are plenty of open plains, but expect a rough touchdown," Sargin warned.

***

A short while later, we exited our craft onto a rugged plain.

Malah handed me a pistol and ammunition clips. A scope was attached to it. "You will need this," he said. Pistols were familiar to me, but only for target practice, never for defense.

Sargin and the pilot set some explosives with a delayed timer. Once we were safely away, the explosives detonated, destroying our useless craft.

Enkidu, who had fallen back after our takeoff from Ganteep City, arrived and circled above, keeping a watch on us as we began our trek.

CHAPTER 13
LATE AFTERNOON

We hadn't traveled long before the sounds of commotion filled our ears. With each step we took toward our destination, the shrieks of terror and wails of sorrow grew louder amidst the whirring of aircrafts. My hand darted for my holstered pistol when a vessel buzzed by dangerously close. Noting that we weren't in immediate danger, we crept to the edge of a high cliff, surveying the valley below, investigating the source of the noises.

Reptilian infiltrators whipped back and forth, corralling giants who were scurrying to find escape. At the far end of the valley along a tree line, troop transports landed. Reptilian soldiers scampered down the ramps and attacked giants with kukri knives, the blades of which resembled small machetes. Enkidu soared overhead, but the reptilians paid him no mind. They were preoccupied, almost joyfully, with their prey.

"I want to go," I pleaded.

"What are they doing?" Malah wondered, undeterred by my request.

"They are hunting," Hazi answered.

"Wouldn't it be easier to just use their aircraft to decimate the land?" Malah pointed out.

Hazi rested her chin in her palm. "I'm guessing the reptilians are culling for food."

We watched three more transport ships land.

"Food?" I asked, nauseated with the thought.

Hazi dropped her hand, pushing her torso upward. "This place is a smorgasbord for them," she muttered.

"Where are we again?" I asked. "Land of what?"

Captain Malah slung his weapon. "The Land of Darmant, Keiji," he answered. He lifted an eyebrow toward Hazi. "This is one of the places Hazi's people like to hunt."

Hazi rolled her eyes. "Giants are beasts," she answered, gritting her teeth. "Now let's go."

We scooted our way off the cliff, then began our hike through the brush. Our point man, one of the surviving soldiers, monitored a scanner that led us toward the signal Sargin had mentioned earlier.

"Keiji," said the doctor, in my head.

Without speaking, I answered, *Where have you been?*

"I have been with you the entire time," he answered.

What is going on? I asked. *What is all this craziness?*

"The end of the world," the doctor answered. "We sent you to the end of the Second Age, right before the apocalypse."

And you're telling me this now? You basically sent me to my death! I grunted.

"No," the doctor shot back, "we will get you out of there. If we had not sent you to a time in which nearly everything and everyone was annihilated, then all your actions could have disastrous effects to the timeline. But since nearly everybody is about to die, you really can't do much harm."

An overwhelming sense of loss sent shivers down my spine as I recalled the screams in my head each time the three dragons died.

Did I hear those dragons in my head as they were killed? I asked.

"I believe you were connected somehow," the doctor replied with a consoling tone. "It's fortunate that one dragon remains with you. I am hoping you can build a telepathic bridge with him."

I scanned the skies where Enkidu circled, without attracting any attention to himself. The reptilian ships ignored the flying creature.

Does the dragon hear me? I asked.

"I'm not sure," the doctor admitted, "but I hope so, or this whole endeavor is for naught."

You're wanting me to communicate with the dragon? I asked with skepticism.

"If you can. Let's not focus on that right now," the doctor redirected. "I'm detecting Midlatican technology on you."

Midlatican? Not Ganteep? I lifted my wrist to see the bracelet Malah had given me. *This bracelet allows me to pass through force fields.*

"It does more than that," the doctor added. "My ability to track you has cleared up considerably since you put that thing on."

"Keiji," called Hazi, "pick up the pace!"

"I'll let you focus, Keiji," the doctor said. "Remember: when you get a chance, try to communicate with the dragon."

His name is Enkidu, I thought.

"Enkidu," the doctor confirmed.

I heard a mechanical switch flip off in my head, letting me know my conversation with the doctor had ceased.

A hand on my back nudged me forward. It was the soldier who was taking up the rear position. He kept a watchful eye on our surroundings. "What's your name?" I asked.

"Sayce," he answered with a whisper.

"Nice to meet you," I greeted.

Sayce only nodded, keeping his attention to the landscape around us. I sized up Sayce from head to toe. He looked about my age, but he was more than likely several times older than me. He kept pace with ease, maintaining a lookout for any harm from behind.

It was getting more difficult to walk through the dense undergrowth, while above, trees rose with a canopy of wet, gleaming leaves. A family of monkeys leaped from one tree to the other, dropping half-eaten fruit. Colorful birds followed our movements. The howling of monkeys, hooting of birds, and flapping of wings filled our ears. Occasional glimpses revealed animals familiar in my time, but here they were larger and nimbler.

I stumbled on one of the rocks and fell. A soldier helped me up. "I am Tell-Brah," the soldier said, without a prompt.

"Thank you, Tell-Brah," I said. "Who is the one leading us at the front?" I asked, wiping the dirt off my pants.

"That's Malbim," he answered.

"Are you the one in charge?" I asked him, noticing an insignia that displayed more branches on it than the other soldiers.

"I'm their squad leader."

"It was your squad then, that mounted the skiff," I confirmed. Tell-Brah nodded.

"So many of them lost their lives helping us," I acknowledged.

Tell-Brah maintained a polished appearance and demeanor. "Their sacrifices should be celebrated. Their loyalties never wavered from their duties to the king."

I thought about King Sar and the ghastly explosion that swept him away in Ganteep City. "But the king has died," I stated. "Does that sever your commitment in any way?"

Malah turned his head back over his shoulder, listening to our conversation.

Tell-Brah, brandishing his weapon, gestured to Sargin. "We still have a king," he corrected, "and we have a mission to get you to Midlatica to retrieve that scroll." Tell-Brah glowed with pride and purpose.

"I guess you do," I said. "Speaking of which, who's the guy that flew us out of Ganteep?"

"Don't know," Tell-Brah answered. "Go ask him."

I caught up with Sargin, who was whispering to his fellow pilot.

"This is Ningal," Sargin said, introducing me to his companion.

"Impressive flying and smooth landing," I kidded.

Ningal gave me a quizzical look. "Smooth? I'd classify that as a crash landing," he joked. "It's Enkidu we need to thank. He and his sons gave us the protection we needed to take off."

His sons?

I realized an awful truth. It wasn't the dragons I sensed dying but, rather, the cries from Enkidu. I dropped to one knee, overwhelmed with the cringing emotions.

"What's wrong, Keiji?" Malah asked, kneeling beside me.

"Back at the airfield, when Enkidu's sons were killed, I heard Enkidu scream in my head," I said.

Malah took hold of my arm. "Could you hear Enkidu's thoughts?"

"More like, felt his thoughts," I said, trying to give a closer approximation. "Maybe I picked up his feelings. It's hard to explain."

Malah helped me to my feet.

"Can you feel Enkidu now?" Malah asked. I sensed his tight bond with the dragon.

I closed my eyes and tried to reach out to Enkidu, but I sensed nothing. "No."

Malbim interjected, lifting his sensor for Malah to see. "It's detecting ships landing nearby."

"Any infiltrators?" Malah asked.

"Just transports with about three dozen lifeforms." Malbim furrowed his brow, shaking the sensor. "Wait a minute." We scanned the horizon, watching the transport Malbim detected take off.

"Did they just drop off something and leave?" I asked.

"Looks like it," Malbim said, adjusting a few dials on the device. "I don't recommend waiting to find out what they left behind."

"Probably a hunting party in search of more giants. If we don't move fast, they may hunt for us too," Hazi warned.

My stomach tightened with fear.

Captain Malah turned to Tell-Brah. "We need to hurry,"

"My father fought reptilians in the past," Sargin explained, "and if they capture us, they will kill us, store our bodies somewhere underwater to tenderize us, and then eat us."

I winced at Sargin's vivid depiction. I pulled my gun out of the holster. "Let's get out of here," I urged, wanting to put as much distance as possible between us and the reptilians.

Chapter 14
NEARING DUSK

Malah and I lay behind a rock under the concealment of branches, trying to examine the approaching enemy. He pulled a handgun scope out and peered through it. With the addition of a shoulder piece, the gun could be converted to a rifle with a scope. The soldiers with this weapon never bothered removing the scope when in pistol form.

"Yeah, I can see them," Malah whispered, fatigued from the encroaching pursuit. "Hold on."

With my scope, I watched the scene below. Reptilian soldiers encircled a giant with brown braids, jabbing at him with metal poles. The giant towered over them, but their weapons were more effective despite his larger size. With each strike, the giant squawked or yelped. He lunged forward to grab hold of the smaller creatures, but they hopped away from danger with ease.

The reptilians wore a tight-fitting dark-blue uniform, armed with pistols, mini blasters, and a baton-like weapon. Kukri knives were sheathed in scabbards, strapped across their chests.

Ridges protruded from the tops of their skulls. Their noses were nothing more than two nostrils above their gaping mouths. They blinked against the sunset, revealing catlike golden irises.

The giant swung his arms in panic toward one of the grayish creatures but missed. A reptilian bashed the giant in the back of the head with a baton, flinging the braids over the giant's face and knocking him to his knees. Other reptilians pummeled at him with their own batons, knocking him over and pinning him to the ground. They unsheathed their knives and sliced into the giant, removing chunks of flesh. Hastily, the creatures consumed the fresh meat. The giant could only watch and scream in horror.

"They are eating him alive," I managed, covering my mouth with repulsion.

A larger reptilian looked on, monitoring the activity around him. This reptilian appeared calmer and more collected. His skull ridges were larger and more defined. His uniform was decked out with paraphernalia, denoting a superior rank.

A smaller reptilian offered him pieces of meat, but he refused. His attention was focused on a short-haired giant that lay on a bed of gravel, writhing in pain. The elder reptilian pulled out a kukri and ripped through the giant's throat. The giant's body ceased moving, and the gravel turned red, soaked by the leaking blood.

A spear ripped through the air, startling the reptilians. They snapped their heads toward the source, discovering a giant sprinting toward them, holding a tree branch. The elder reptilian, with a weapon still in hand, sprinted to confront the attacker. He made quick work of the giant by slicing down and up. The giant's body dropped to the ground, blood pouring from his arms and chest. He tried to lift himself up, but the elder sliced his neck. The giant grabbed his throat and gurgled to his death.

The elder promptly gave orders. Without delay, reptilians attached round metal tags to fallen prey, levitating them and then pushing them into transport ships scattered throughout the field.

I zoomed in with my scope and made a startling discovery. The reptilians hadn't only preyed on mature male giants. "Women and children," I muttered. My muscles quivered with tension at the unsettling sight.

"What?" Hazi asked, taking a position between Malah and me. She grabbed my scope to see for herself. A tear streamed down her face, which she brushed away with her forearm. "I thought giants were only males." she said.

"Why?" I asked.

"Because we believed that they take human women to bear them sons," she explained.

Thoughts of the legendary bigfoot and yeti came to my mind. Many believed they existed, but few, if any, had ever seen one. I always imagined that if they existed, they could only survive if there were males and females to reproduce. Hazi's surprise at the existence of female giants felt absurd to me.

Malah brushed my shoulder, interrupting my thoughts. "I think they're looking our way," he said, pointing downward.

Through my scope I could see the elder gaze upward in our direction. His eyes shot from left to right. He blinked while pulling out a device from his belt and spat some orders. Reptilians grouped themselves into four squads, each with their weapons brandished, and they marched forward.

"They know we're here," warned Malah.

"Then we need to get out of here," Hazi growled.

"They are faster than us," Malah grumbled but offered no alternative.

"How far is the crash site?" I asked, not willing to give up.

"If they can track us, it won't matter," Malah said. "They can outpace us, so we'll have to make a stand and fight!"

I dug my nails into the dirt, frustrated with Malah's response.

"Keiji," the doctor called into my head.

"What?" I blurted aloud. Malah and Hazi tilted their heads with curiosity. I tapped my fingers to my temples, indicating I was speaking to the doctor. They stared with widened eyes in anticipation for some hopeful information.

"I am going to send you an update to the software in the bracelets."

How are you going to do that? I asked, sliding down backward from my observation station.

"Just tell everyone to put their bracelets on your skull," he instructed.

You're kidding me, right? I asked, trying to imagine everyone piling on top of each other to press their wrists to my head.

"No," the doctor chuckled.

"Hey, everybody," I said, crawling to the rest of the team with Malah and Hazi in tow under the concealment of vegetation. "The doctor wants to alter the programming to our bracelets."

"What kind of alteration?" Sargin asked.

The doctor answered in my head. "I am going to hide your life signatures, so the reptilians can't detect you."

"It's going to make us undetectable to the reptilians, so place your wrists on my head," I relayed, liking the idea. Everyone gathered around and followed my instructions.

Feeling awkward, I sighed. "We are good to go, Doctor."

"Hold on," ordered the doctor, "and ... now!"

My head felt like I was pressed against a live spark plug, causing me to yelp. Everybody apparently felt the same sensation as they quickly pulled their wrists away and babied them in their hands.

"For crying out loud," Tell-Brah whispered in anguish.

Hazi grinned, combing my hair with her hand. "Your hair is sticking straight up."

Malah grabbed his scope and climbed back up to the rock. "Check this out."

I joined Malah. Below, the reptilians took a knee, forming a perimeter around a smaller group. Those in the center shook the instruments in their hands.

"Well, I'll be a Midlatican," Malah huffed. "It worked!"

"They may not pick us up with scanners, but I hear reptilians are efficient trackers," Hazi warned with pessimism.

"I'll take point," Malbim volunteered, taking the scanner from Ningal's hand.

The air cracked above as Enkidu flapped his wings.

"Enkidu may lead them right to us," Malah said.

"Send the dragon away," the doctor ordered.

"But—" I protested.

"Just do it!" he commanded with a raised voice. "Use your mind."

I closed my eyes, picturing Enkidu in my mind and tried projecting my thoughts to him. At first, I felt nothing and was about to give up when my body flushed with warmth. I opened my eyes and watched Enkidu fly away.

Where to? I had no idea.

CHAPTER 15
EVENING

Malbim took another reading from his scanner. "We should be there in no time," he informed us.

I froze at the snap of a branch that sounded as if it were only a dozen or so yards away. My heart pounded as I tried to find the source of the noise. It was difficult to see in the darkness. In the center of the evening sky, one object appeared abnormally bright, which I assumed was the fast-approaching moon.

Hazi eased down to her knee, scouting out our flank. I edged closer to her. She pressed a finger to her lips, signaling me to remain silent, while focusing her attention on a thicket of brush. Something interested her, but I witnessed no movement. A light wind blew through the trees, rustling the leaves all around.

Consternation struck me when three reptilian soldiers worked their way through the brush, oblivious to us. They crept by us only a few yards away, making no sound. One of them stopped, stuck out his tongue like a lizard, and sniffed the air. Blades were sheathed in each of his knee-high boots. A holster strapped around his thigh held a mini blaster. He gripped a pistol in one hand and clutched his baton in the other.

I held my breath in anticipation, trying to avoid detection. The reptilian walked upwind past us, his odor a distinct dust-like smell. He, along with his two companions, moved on until out of sight, and our party sighed in relief.

"Whew," Sayce gasped. One second later, Sayce lurched. I fell back in shock at the sight of a kukri knife protruding from Sayce's chest with blood gushing out. Behind Sayce, large black eyes blinked.

Hazi launched an arrow into the slit nostrils of the reptilian, sending it floundering backward to the feet of two other reptilian soldiers, crouched and ready for combat. One of them flung a dagger into Malbim's chest, piercing through his body armor like it was butter. Malbim collapsed.

Tell-Brah lunged at the reptilian closest to him. He grappled with the gray creature, trying to prevent it from grabbing a blade. The reptilian struck Tell-Brah in the head with his elbow. Then, armed with a kukri, he attempted to slice at Tell-Brah, but the Ganteep guard pulled out his pistol and fired, detaching much of the creature's cranium with a single shot.

Ningal deflected an attack from his assailant, but the creature swung a blade quickly, slicing Ningal's jaw. Stunned, he reached for his face, but the creature swept his legs out from under him, knocking his head into a tree with a splatter.

Gunshot blasts erupted into my ears and echoed throughout the valley. Malah unloaded several rounds into a reptilian's torso and, for a final measure, put a bullet in the creature's eye.

I raced to Ningal to try to help, but his lungs had already shut down. Blood dripped down the tree trunk, pooling around him. Knowing there was nothing I could do, I rushed to Malbim, but he lay on his back, unmoving, with eyes open and unfocused. The dagger was still embedded in his chest.

Malah grabbed my shoulder. "We have to go," he whispered.

I turned to acknowledge Malah, but panic washed over me upon spotting the three reptilians who passed us earlier. They trotted toward us. Adrenaline surged through my veins, replacing my panic. My pupils dilated, enhancing my ability to see. My other senses were heightened also. The adrenaline's effects caused me to see the reptilians rush through the brush with more clarity, but their movements were like sludge, as if time had slowed.

Sargin reached for the scanner, took a quick reading, waved his hand in the direction indicated on the device, and ran. The rest of our party followed, running and tripping through the brush as we fled our pursuers.

I raised my arms, shielding my face from twigs and slapping branches. My heart pounded in my ringing ears, and my lungs desperately sought oxygen. The ringing softened, only to be replaced by the sounds of a waterfall.

With a new surge of adrenaline, I quickened my pace but remained careful not to trip on any branches or roll my ankle on loose rocks.

Hazi sprinted ahead and, without hesitation, jumped, disappearing below. Sargin reached the edge of the cliff and followed her. Malah did the same. Tell-Brah trudged behind with difficulty, the snarls of reptilians growing louder.

We skidded to a halt when we reached the edge of the cliff. To our right, water fell to the depths below where starlight bounced off crashing water and mist.

"This is madness," I said, apprehensive of making such a jump into the unknown.

The thunderclap of a semiautomatic weapon startled me.

"Go and don't look back!" Tell-Brah yelled, pushing me over the cliff.

Holding my breath, I feared being crushed by a boulder. All I could do was stiffen my body to hit the water like a falling torpedo, hoping it was deep enough.

Those concerns were gone when I plunged into the river. My feet nudged the rocky bottom, letting me know that I survived the jump, but my relief was only temporary. Water currents tossed me around like a ragdoll, and I could not establish my bearings. I reached out to grab anything, but all my efforts were in vain. I fought the urge to breathe in a lungful of water.

A hand grabbed my tunic, pulling me to the surface into fresh air. I gasped. Hazi, with a firm hold on my collar, dragged me to shore. Coughing at first, my body relaxed, and my breathing steadied.

The water splashed. I grabbed my pistol and jumped to my feet, fearing a reptilian water attack. My companions did the same.

We waited, but nothing.

Movement above captured my attention. At the top of the cliff, two reptilians gathered, pondering their next move. Water dripped from my hair into my eyes, but I kept still, trying not to do anything that would attract attention. A few moments later, the two silhouettes were joined by three more.

One of them pointed to the right at the waterfall and barked an order. All five disappeared.

My heart leaped again from a nearby splashing. Someone broke the surface, slapping water and coughing. I pointed my pistol at him but then recognized Tell-Brah.

Hazi dove into the water and brought Tell-Brah to safety. He moaned, grasping at a nub where his arm had been. His eyes bulged from the pain. Blood poured from the gaping wound. Instead of screaming out, he bared his teeth, clenching his shoulder, trying to stop the bleeding. Tell-Brah had received a death sentence.

Sargin knelt by Tell-Brah, unfastened a medical pouch from his belt, injected him with some pain medication, and dressed his wound. Blood soaked the dressing, so in futility, Sargin applied pressure with his hand.

"You should see the other guy," Tell-Brah coughed. "Got to me just as you jumped. I got a bullet in him, but one of the others grabbed my arm and swung his blade."

"Explains why we only saw two up there at first, and not three," Hazi said.

Above the waterfall, the reptilian quintet crossed the river by hopping on rocks.

We moved out with Hazi in the lead. Tell-Brah heaved, trying to keep up, but his injury diminished his ability to maintain momentum. His strength waned. As if paralyzed, Tell-Brah stopped and fell. I knelt by his side and grabbed his good arm.

"No," he resisted while panting. "You have to keep going."

Malah, Hazi, and Sargin joined me. "I'll carry you," Sargin offered.

"No!" Tell-Brah pulled out his weapon. "I'll hold them off as long as I can."

Malah grabbed Tell-Brah's uninjured shoulder. "You did well," he said, giving the soldier a firm grasp.

Sargin placed his hand on Tell-Brah's cheek "I will remember you," Sargin said.

With a mixture of horror and pride, Tell-Brah smiled at Sargin. "Thank you, my King."

Hesitant at first to abandon our comrade, we sprinted away, trying to make up for lost time.

Behind us, the air erupted with the sound of Tell-Brah's weapon, but just as fast, the sound ceased only to be followed by a blood curdling cry. I'd heard that sound before from the giants in the valley.

My adrenaline waned, leaving my legs weak and wobbly. We cleared the woodland and sprinted across an open field. Branches snapped behind us, and I turned back to see four reptilians. Tell-Brah's last stand must have thinned out their party by at least one.

We raced into the clearing, but additional reptilians appeared from the forest line.

Forcing my tired legs forward, I heard oncoming footsteps snapping the underbrush behind us getting closer. "We're not going to make it," I screamed, then saw a spear thrown from the trees in my direction.

Ducking, I looked back to see two reptilians impaled by the single spear.

The remaining pursuers froze, along with the rest of my party. The trees rustled, parting like a curtain, and the starlight revealed a familiar giant wearing a bandage around his eye and holding a shield in his hand. It was Baugi!

Baring his teeth, Baugi screamed and hurled himself toward the reptilians. They pulled out their weapons and discharged them, but their bullets could not penetrate his shield. The foremost attacker dropped an empty magazine and was about to reload when Baugi rammed him in the chest with the shield.

The reptilian attackers pulled out their long knives. One hissed just before an arrow bore through his skull. A second reptilian spotted Hazi but was too late. She had already released an arrow from her bow, drilling through his eye.

Baugi retrieved his spear from the two impaled victims, then crushed one of his attackers with a deadly stomp to the abdomen.

Malah shot a reptilian in the chest. The hot shell casing from the bullet ejected out of the chamber, struck me in the neck, and dropped down my shirt. I slapped at my chest, trying to rid myself of the hot object, as though trying to brush off a bee.

Sargin, holding a pistol with both hands, fired but missed his target. The reptilian opened his mouth, surprised he was still alive. "I'm a better pilot than a marksman," Sargin yelled at the reptilian.

Baugi grabbed the distracted reptilian and swung him into a rock, decapitating him.

One rival remained. I recognized him as the elder reptilian.

Sargin whipped his pistol around, but the reptilian slapped it away, then punched Sargin in the chest. Baugi followed with a swing of his shield, but the reptilian ducked.

Hazi, with an arrow in hand, rammed it into the elder's shoulder, knocking him to the ground. He moaned. She pulled out her spear and jabbed it toward the reptilian's chest. "Vile serpent," she said with toxicity in her voice.

The creature twisted his face with surprise. "What did you call me?"

CHAPTER 16
LATE EVENING

Hazi stumbled backward, shocked with what she heard. Malah pointed his weapon at the injured foe, allowing him to crawl to a tree stump and prop himself up. The starlight, which was brighter than I had remembered in my time, reflected off his face.

"Vile, eh?" he barked, sitting perfectly still to show no threatening gestures.

Hazi sucked air through her teeth. "This thing is talking to me," she blurted with astonishment.

Sargin edged in close to the creature, shining a flashlight in his face, causing his yellow eyes to contract even more. "These monsters killed my people," he spat.

The reptilian pulled the arrow out of his shoulder, wincing in pain. "That's why I'm vile?" he asked, allowing his voice to trail off.

"You're vile because of the attack," Hazi explained, tapping her spear into his wound, inflicting more pain, and causing him to hunch over, "not to mention eating your victims while they are still alive."

"Well," the reptilian began, shrugging his uninjured shoulder, "alive *and* kicking. That's how younglings prefer their food. "

"Baugi hears your words," the giant growled, "but doesn't understand."

The party whipped their heads around to the giant, in shock. Baugi grunted, then hunched over the reptilian and sniffed. "Vile serpent," he repeated. He straightened his back and turned to Hazi. "You took my eye."

Hazi froze at the giant's words.

I was becoming acutely aware that this kind of communication between these races may be unprecedented.

The reptilian slowed his breathing, then met my eyes. "It's you, huh?"

I backed away, stunned.

Malah clutched his weapon. "Yes," he said, unexpectedly. "What of it?"

"More than words, it appears," the reptilian said, minimizing his movement.

"Shouldn't we be killing this thing instead of talking to it?" Sargin mused, hands up. "Heck! Even the giant is trying to put words together. What's next?"

I concentrated my thoughts on the reptilian. "I sense no deceit," I said.

"He was feasting on those giants," Hazi pointed out, not letting her guard down.

"It's fresh meat," he said, licking his chops. "Nom, nom, nom, nom."

Sargin shook his head. "Stop salivating."

"Not you," the reptilian said. "Too many bones. Oh no, no, no, no."

Sargin twisted his face in confusion. "I don't recall ever being so pleasantly insulted."

"Let me guess. The bigger the better, eh?" Hazi speculated to the serpent.

The reptilian looked away. "I'm not a chubby chaser."

Baugi grunted at the reptilian's response. "I don't blame them for their instincts," he said to Hazi. "You're no better."

Hazi spun around, pointing her spear at the hulking man. "What do you mean?"

Baugi cowered back, protecting his one good eye. "You sell my people as food."

"I do not!" Hazi defended herself. "Your people are taken to a preserve where your violence is controlled."

"That preserve was a place to *preserve* food," Baugi said, posing childlike, still protecting his remaining good eye. "Reptilians, disguised as humans, were the ones buying them from you. When my people learned about what was happening, I traveled beyond the Land of Darmant in search for help."

"The giant's correct," the reptilian said with both hands up in defense. "We've been here a long time. Herding and feasting."

Annoyed, Sargin said, "I still think we should kill him!"

"That puny halfwit wants to kill me," the reptilian said, jabbing his thumb toward Sargin, but speaking to the rest of us with sarcasm. "Now that's scary."

The doctor interrupted my attention. "Don't let them kill the reptilian," he said.

"Why not?" I asked out loud. Everyone turned their attention to me.

"He should not understand you," the doctor explained. "My scanners are picking up a brainwave pattern that I've never seen before in any reptilian."

The reptilian coughed. "Is he a mental case?" he asked, nudging his head toward me. "Why is he talking to himself?"

Hazi pressed the spear into his wound again. "Shut your trap, or I'll shut it for you."

"Whatever," the reptilian grunted in defiance.

Baugi stepped in and roared at the reptilian, who in turn wiped the spit off his face. "This imbecile is giving away your position," he chuckled, belittling the giant.

Malah cuffed the reptilian, forcing him to his feet. Hazi stripped him of his weapons, then shoved him back to the ground. In hindsight, we should have stripped him of his weapons first, but the sudden ability to communicate stunned us. The reptilian snarled at her. "Those giants you sold us are in water tanks, tenderizing nicely to be a great feast for us older ones," he taunted, showing off some of the reptilian anger still within him.

Hazi slapped him across the face with her bow.

Baugi let out a lungful of air, shaking his head in disgust, but not angry with the reptilian. The frustration was directed to Hazi, and she knew it. "Keiji," the doctor called. "Just put your bracelet on the reptilian's head."

Are you out of your mind? I asked. *I'm not going to touch him.* I turned to Baugi in panic.

The gargantuan man, as if reading my mind, suddenly grabbed the reptilian by the neck, restraining the creature who squealed in pain.

I rushed over and did as I was instructed. *Okay. I have it on his head*, I informed the doctor.

The bracelet shot a spark, causing the reptilian to shudder, then go limp. Baugi let him go.

What happened? I asked.

Everyone stood around me, just as shocked.

"I accelerated his evolution," the doctor said. "Don't kill him. Trust me. This is important."

I turned to everyone. "The doctor says we can't kill him," I said, holding my arms out wide. "Apparently, this one's evolving."

The reptilian whistled, waking up. "I see fireflies," he said, reaching out into thin air.

We stared down at him, giving quizzical looks. There were no fireflies.

"Oh look," the reptilian said, pointing at nothing. "I think they like each other." He smiled, swinging his arm like he was conducting an orchestra.

"Are you sure he isn't de-evolving?" Sargin asked.

"I have no idea," I responded, dumbfounded.

The reptilian then turned to me. He looked drugged. "I saw your dragon," the reptilian claimed, cracking a grin, "and felt him." He chuckled.

Malah stroked his chin. "You felt the dragon?" he asked rhetorically, then tossed his head, as if shaking off a gnat.

"He's delusional," Sargin said. "Maybe we can get some information out of him."

Malah stepped closer to the reptilian. "Why are you here?"

"Why am I here?" the reptilian asked back, misunderstanding the question, but did not wait before answering. "I volunteered for one last hurrah before the Maktar'Mak test," he blubbered. "If you don't pass, the younglings get to eat you. I'll tell you a secret," he leaned in and whispered. "I wasn't expecting to pass," he admitted, in a drunken state. "What a meal I was to be for them, eh?"

Sargin crouched next to the reptilian. "What's your name?"

"Andros," he answered, then his face stiffened as if suddenly sober. "Commander Andros."

"Okay, Commander Andros," Sargin said with sarcasm, snapping his fingers to get his attention. "The ones that pass the test. What are they like?"

"Zealots. They believe in reptilian supremacy," Andros said excitedly, managing to fight the pain and pump out his chest with dominance, then crossed his eyes and slumped back, grasping at invisible fireflies again.

Malah whispered into my ear. "Did the doctor make him bipolar?"

"More like tripolar," I said. "He is definitely not playing with a full deck."

"This is not an exact science," the doctor admitted, overhearing our conversation. "Just give him some time."

I relayed the doctor's request to the group.

Sargin scratched his jaw. "Well, we should always do what the doctor orders."

Hazi walked up to the giant. "My heart broke when I saw the women and children try to flee the ravages of the reptilian attacks."

Baugi raised his hand to his missing eye. "You took Baugi's eye," he said. "Why Baugi's eye?"

Hazi raked her fingers through her hair, flinging the braids behind her shoulders. She pointed to me. "This is Keiji, the traveler. He needs help," she said. "King Sar offered to grant any request of mine if I defeated you in battle. It was either kill you or maim you."

Baugi lifted his hand and slowly extended his index finger at me. "It was you," he said. "It was you who put the image in my head at the arena."

My mouth gaped open with the realization that I was successful. "It was," I affirmed.

"You saved my life," Baugi said. "What do you seek?"

"A Kantara Scroll," Hazi answered for me.

Andros struggled to his feet. "In case you're interested, there are at least twenty reptilian raiders behind us. They are all younglings!" He began fumbling with a Midlatican bracelet. "How do I put this thing on and activate it?" he asked.

"Give me that," Malah said, snatching the bracelet out of Andros's hand, knowing it came from one of his dead soldiers.

"Are you an idiot?" Andros asked. "They can track me unless I wear that bracelet too."

Malah gave a blank face, not willing to be swayed by any of the reptilian's reasoning. "That bracelet belonged to one of my men."

"I know," Andros said, blinking, then waved his hand. "Whatever. We don't have much time."

"Explain again why we aren't killing him?" Malah asked, then grabbed his gear.

CHAPTER 17
NIGHT

Baugi led the way, taking directions from Sargin, whipping through the brush and leaving a trail for us to follow. Hazi kept her spear trained on Andros. The injured reptilian found it difficult to keep up with the rest of the group.

"What are we supposed to do with him?" Malah asked Sargin, huffing. "He's going to slow us down."

"I know," Sargin said, elbowing his way through some branches. "What did the doctor do to him anyway?" he asked me.

I held my hand to my temple, listening to the doctor's response, then relayed the message. "He just downloaded some reprogramming," I said. "They've tried it with other reptilian test subjects before without success. Something about Andros is different."

"That sounds like a useless response," Sargin remarked, rolling his eyes.

"Test subjects?" Andros asked from behind us.

"Listen," Malah snapped at Andros. "You need to shut your ugly face up."

"You're delicious," Andros snarled back. I sensed that Andros was only taunting Malah out of anger.

Malah lifted his eyebrows, wrinkling his forehead. He was about to respond when Andros cut him off. "What's your name?" Andros addressed his question to me.

"Keiji," I answered with no fear.

Andros widened his stride to walk next to me, but Hazi grabbed Andros by the collar and pulled him back. "Not too close," she warned.

Andros clenched his jaw from the pain in his shoulder. "Keiji," he said, feeling the relief of pain subsiding. "Those test subjects may have been younglings. It wouldn't work on them. Their brains work off instinct, not logic."

The doctor chimed in. "The reptilian may have a point. Maybe it works on Andros because he is older."

"You seem to know very little about them," I said out loud to the doctor.

Andros pointed to his skull. "So he's talking to the guy in his head?" he asked Hazi, flicking his tongue.

Sargin pressed a finger to his lips, wanting us to stay quiet.

"My readings on Andros show that his brain has evolved considerably in the past few minutes," the doctor informed me. "My programming is working."

"Andros turned pretty fast," I whispered. Glancing at his reptilian skin, oversized features, and nostril slits, he appeared very alien. Despite these differences, I could see humanity in his soft expression.

"We did something similar to you, and it might work if you really did send Enkidu away with your mind," the doctor admitted. "If you can take the next step and communicate with the dragon, our mission has a great chance of success."

"What's so important about the dragon?" I asked, grumbling.

"Are you done talking?" Malah whispered harshly.

I gave Malah my apologies and heard a click in my head, which signaled the doctor severing his discussion with me. He didn't answer my question.

We trekked along in the dark for a while with only rustling leaves and insect songs disturbing the quiet. Occasionally, we used flashlights, but the bright stars twinkling above, unobstructed by any clouds, usually provided us with enough light to navigate through the forest. The trees, rising out of the brush, flickered shadows onto the ground. Twice, fallen trees blocked our path, forcing us to climb over them.

The snap of a branch echoed from behind. We froze. I concentrated to ascertain if I could gain any insight of what was behind us, but short of the group around me, I sensed nothing.

Another branch snapped, but this time, it was louder. Our pursuers were closing the gap. The muscles in my body tensed, and with the next branch that snapped, we darted forward.

Sargin led us through the woods. Baugi, who was just ahead of me, crushed and pounded the underbrush.

"This way," Sargin said, waving his hand, but then tripped down a hill.

Sargin rolled, unable to stop, while figures below sprinted up toward him.

Andros quickly slipped his hands free of the cuffs, pulled his kukri blade from Hazi's belt, and leaped after Sargin. Hazi chased after Andros, fearful he'd attack the prince. What happened, though, was a shock, even with my empathic ability.

Andros hurled his body into a newly exposed attacker, then thrust his head upward, knocking his opponent to the ground. With his kukri blade in hand, he swung outward, slicing the reptilian's midsection.

One of the other reptilians witnessed the incident and bared his teeth in recognition. "I will feast on you, Andros," he screamed. His words translated perfectly for all of us to hear. He lunged an attack at Andros, but Hazi struck first, decapitating the attacker with her spear.

Sargin collapsed at the bottom of the hill but, like a spring, jumped up with a pistol in hand and fired. Malah, who raced down the hill after Hazi, reached Sargin and joined him in shooting the attackers. Andros, meanwhile, sliced and diced his fellow reptilians.

An attacker chased after Andros from behind. He pulled his kukri to attack, but Baugi appeared from the brush and grabbed the reptilian by the chest, throwing him into the nearest tree, dismembering him.

While fending off another reptilian soldier, Andros lost his balance but regained it in time to block a downward thrust of an opposing kukri knife. The weapons entangled. With a twisting motion, Andros tripped his opponent, and they rolled into a tree. Andros whipped himself around on all fours and, using the ridges in his head, thrust himself into the enemy, penetrating his chest. A short scream later, the reptilian went limp. Andros dislodged his cranium from his victim.

I joined my party, albeit too late to be of any assistance, and held my weapon, listening for any other pursuers. I sensed nothing.

Sargin checked his scanner, pushed a few buttons, shook it, and tossed it to the ground. "The scanner broke during the fall," he informed us. "Finding the crash under these circumstances is next to impossible." With anger, he turned to me. "I'm telling you that you really need to shut up!" He looked around at the rest of the party, mouth trembling in anger. "All of you just need to learn to shut up."

"That's not how they are tracking us," said Andros. "They can smell my blood." He fell to the ground. "The wind has changed. Personally, I'm a little disappointed in our reptilian pursuers. Between the gargantuan trampling through the brush, Keiji's loud mouth, and the smell of blood, we should have been picked off a long time ago."

Sargin let out a deep huff, ignoring the reptilian's words of insight. Baugi caught his attention. "That crash you were in. You know where it is, don't you?" Sargin asked.

"Baugi crashed!" Baugi said, shaking his head.

There was a click in my mind, letting me know that the doctor was listening in again.

"Baugi. Do you know where the crash is?" Sargin asked again.

Baugi nodded. "I think so. I got out before it crashed."

"How did you get out?" Hazi asked.

"A man pushed me," he said.

"Who?" I asked.

Baugi shrugged. "Don't know. He just gave me my stuff and a blanket on strings," he said. I assumed the blanket was a parachute.

Sargin then waved to get my attention. "Does the bracelet need to be on the wearer for the doctor to do his thing? Hide his life signs?" he asked, holding up the Midlatican bracelet that Malah confiscated from Andros.

After a short exchange with the doctor, I answered with affirmation.

Sargin snapped the bracelet on him.

"Have the doctor do that thing with your head," Sargin ordered. I reached out to the doctor, and within moments, the bracelet on Andros's wrist was hiding his life signs.

"Should slow them for now if they are picking him up," I said, hoping.

"Not if they smell my blood," Andros corrected.

Malah slapped the cuffs back on Andros. "Not that these do much good, but I feel better with them on." The reptilian teetered from signs of weakness and collapsed.

The giant picked up Andros. "Baugi carry lizard man. Baugi will take you to the crash," and with that, he plowed through the next stretch of forest, making our path and direction clear.

CHAPTER 18
PAST MIDNIGHT

Andros slipped in and out of consciousness while Baugi held him. My empathic connection with him was slipping. It felt like Andros was shutting down his body on purpose. The constant moving was beginning to take a toll on my body, but for some reason, I kept feeling my energy renewed, helping me take more steps. In my time, air was filled with pollution and smog. In this time of the Second Age, though, oxygen was plentiful. But the pursuit demanded rest for all of us. We had been running from our pursuers all night.

Sargin waved his hand, wanting us to stop and take a breather. Baugi set Andros down, then plopped onto a boulder. Andros's uniform was drenched with blood from his wound. Hazi remained standing, keeping an eye out while the rest of us took in some water from a creek.

Hazi crept to a clearing to get eyes on the raiders behind. Baugi stayed with Andros while the rest of us joined Hazi. We looked through our pistol scopes, which were set to night vision. The reptilians had taken a parallel path that led them to a wide meadow.

"What do you think?" Sargin asked.

Hazi bit her lower lip. "The wind has changed. Maybe the smell of blood isn't as strong."

"I agree. The bleeding has slowed, and we are downwind," Malah said without putting down his scope. "If we go now and change course, we might lose them."

"We have to get to the craft as fast as we can, or we don't stand a chance," Sargin argued. "We could really use Enkidu's help about now."

I thought I saw the movement of a dragon in the sky, but when I looked up, there appeared to be something else. I widened my eyes, focusing on the object, and saw not one but two objects. I examined them with my scope. "What the ...," I said, my mouth gaping.

Two warcruisers hovered in the distance with blinking lights. Between the ships and the surface, small crafts darted back and forth.

"Looks like they are collecting their spoils of war," Malah muttered. "Spoils, I'm guessing, are mostly food."

Sargin took a deep breath. "I suppose the fun of their hunt is coming to an end," he whispered.

Images from the previous day flooded my brain, and for the first time since the attack, I pondered the scope of the atrocities. The explosion in the city. The infiltrator attacks on the people. The feasting on the giants. I cringed, gripping a clump of hair on my scalp, trying to remove the images from my mind.

Malah laid a gentle hand on my shoulder. "Keiji," he whispered. "It's not the time to grieve."

We rejoined Baugi and the limp Andros and continued our journey through the forest.

Trees creaked in the wind, and the forest grew dense. Roots protruded from the ground, making it more difficult to retain our footing. I slipped on the accumulation of leaves below at one point, falling against a tree and scraping my arm on its bark.

We stopped again to rest, taking the opportunity to set eyes on the reptilian party. They had managed to divert from their parallel vector and found our trail, but they were moving slowly, unsure of our direction.

"The wind is in our favor," Malah said, "so they won't be able to smell us too easily. They can still track us if they see fresh breaks on branches."

"Looks like we opened the gap some," Hazi reassured us, then turned to Baugi. "You ready, big guy?"

Baugi nodded, checked the reptilian's chest wound, and flung Andros like a sack of potatoes over his shoulder. "I know where I am. Follow me," and with that, Baugi raced through the forest.

I tripped on another branch and slammed my knee on the root of a tree. I pounded my fist in the air, trying not to cry out. Hazi, having witnessed my stumble, grabbed my arm and helped me back to my feet. The pain subsided after a few seconds. Hazi placed a kind hand on my back, and I found the energy to run again.

The ground inclined, and the muscles in my legs burned from the upward motion. Baugi walked at a quick pace, forcing us to jog to keep up. Hazi used her spear like a walking stick to help push her forward on several occasions. We reached a point above the trees, and I felt exposed, worried that we could be seen. Finally, Baugi stopped and pointed down into a valley. "Crash," he said.

I fell to my knees, careful not to put too much impact on my bruised one, and let out a sigh of relief. "Finally!"

Beyond the treetops, in an open meadow in the valley, lay a crumpled craft sporting four propellers, warped and bent. It was the same kind of craft in which I was escorted to Ganteep City.

"Perfect," Malah said. "Those have transport vehicles inside. Anytime we leave the city, we load smaller scout crafts that can hold up to three people each."

"Will they hold Baugi?" I asked.

Malah chuckled at a thought that crossed his mind. "Nah, but I have something that will work."

"What will work?" Baugi asked.

"Don't worry about it," Malah said, patting the oversized companion on the leg.

"What are you going to do to Baugi?" Baugi asked.

"Trust me," Malah said with a lopsided grin.

Baugi pouted his lip, groaning with acceptance.

It took nearly an hour to navigate the difficult rocky terrain to the crash site. We approached the craft, the nose of which dug into the ground. Tree branches protruded from the cockpit windows. It was mangled, with the side split open wide enough for a normal size person to squeeze through.

Malah entered and flicked on his flashlight. Sargin and I followed him in. Sargin, being a pilot, was more familiar with the aircraft, so he shined his light upward and found what he was looking for. Two crafts, still secured to the wall of the larger craft, shone like a beacon of hope.

"How did Baugi get out?" Malah asked, looking around to find a hole big enough for Baugi to fit through.

"The crew probably dropped him while still in flight," Sargin speculated.

"He said someone helped him out. Pushed him, I think," I said. "Do you think anyone survived?"

Sargin shrugged his shoulders, then climbed a ladder to the cockpit. Malah inspected the inside of the craft, looking for an exit point. He fixed his gaze on the opening. "I guess we'll have to widen that crack if we are going to get these scout vehicles out of here."

"How can we do that?" I asked, inspecting the opening.

"There should be some explosives somewhere around here," he said, shining his light throughout the interior. He was referring to the same kind of explosives used to destroy the plane that brought us out of Ganteep City. Obviously, nobody was left behind to detonate them here.

"The pilot and crew are dead. In fact, two of them were impaled by branches that breached the cockpit," Sargin confirmed.

I took a sharp breath in, then let the air exit slowly.

Malah refocused our attention by shining his light on the scout vehicles. "Getting these things off the wall should be no problem. We'll need to get to work on opening that hole," he said, emphasizing the need for a plan.

Sargin understood the insinuation by Malah. "I'll find the explosives," Sargin said, "and we'll create a controlled explosion, so we don't destroy our crafts ... or kill ourselves. We will only have one chance to make this work."

"If those reptilians are moving as fast as we think, we may not have time to properly set up for a controlled explosion," Malah warned.

"Then we will buy time by setting up a proper defense," I suggested, looking at Hazi standing outside.

CHAPTER 19

DAWN OF THE FOURTH DAY

We hadn't had an ounce of sleep all night, and now the sun was creeping over the trees, giving us a small glimpse of hope for another day.

Malah and I climbed up toward the cockpit and entered a small compartment with a door and a button panel. Malah punched in a code, which opened the door and exposed a full armory with guns, blasters, and ammunition.

Malah pulled out a minigun-like weapon that resembled a nineteenth-century Gatling gun and cradled it with both arms. "Think Baugi can handle this?" he asked me.

"He'll probably love it," I said, grinning.

Malah handed me the gun, then pulled out several boxes full of ammo belts, and I passed them down the ladder to Sargin, who set them to the side. Malah handed me more items until the armory was empty.

"That should work," Malah said, rubbing his shoulder. "Keiji, go hand out the weapons. I'll get the explosives."

I carried the machine gun and handed it to Baugi. "Do you think you can handle this?" I asked him. Baugi grabbed the gun and inspected it. He twirled the gun, then tried unsuccessfully to put his finger through the trigger guard. "His finger is too big," I yelled back inside to Malah.

Malah slid down the ladder and rushed to our aid. He pulled the weapon from Baugi's hand and dislodged the guard. "How's that?" he asked.

Baugi dropped his shield and took hold of the gun.

Malah and I retrieved more ammo and weapons and took them outside. Hazi and Baugi busied themselves loading their weapons. Once done, they scouted for defensive positions. Meanwhile, Andros rested by the opening, dazed and confused.

"Take Andros inside," Hazi ordered me, peering through the gunsights.

"I think I should help you," I suggested.

She shook her head. "We need to keep you safe," she said. "Baugi and I will take a position at that hill and provide whatever defense we can." She pointed to her left toward the back end of the craft. "When you blast through that hole, we will join you."

Baugi, with gun and ammunition in hand, trotted to the hill, taking a position that gave him a clear view of the path we suspected our pursuers were on. Hazi prepped the area near Baugi to have easy access to various weapons.

Andros looked on, still recuperating. I bent down to assess his condition, trying to determine if I could move him inside. He looked back at me with bulging reptilian eyes. "Are you able to stand?" I asked him. Andros nodded, and without asking, he held out his arm for me to grab. I lent a hand to get him to his feet, and we stepped through the opening in the craft. I helped him down to rest against the wall.

To my left, Malah was placing explosives on the edge of the opening. Directly ahead, Sargin unstrapped the scout vehicles tethered to the inner walls.

One of the scout vehicles broke free and dropped without hitting the ground. Its antigravity technology kept it floating above the surface.

Sargin motioned me forward toward a vehicle with his arm. "Get Andros in there," Sargin directed.

I opened a side door, revealing a single bucket seat for the driver and two seats in the back. With the reptilian's arms wrapped around my neck, I helped him inside. He rested his head on the side window and maintained slow breaths. He appeared to be on the verge of falling unconscious again.

"Are you going to be okay?" I asked, with a hand resting on his uninjured shoulder, but he only grunted. "I'll be right back."

Sargin unstrapped the second vehicle, which dropped and hovered. He jumped in it, pushed some buttons, and flipped a few switches to start the engine, which cycled with a gentle hum. He did the same with the other vessel.

"Baugi's too big for the scouts," I called out to Malah. "What was your bright idea?"

Sargin, who had already discussed this problem with his captain, handed me a belt with four palm-sized cylindrical objects attached to it. "Put this on him."

"What is it?" I asked, retrieving one of the cylinders that fell loose and clamping it back onto the belt.

Sargin pulled out what looked like some form of remote control. "We use these to haul large animals killed in a hunt," he said. He turned away and assisted Malah in preparing the explosives.

I passed by the two men, who were hard at work, and hurried to Baugi. Hazi lay on the opposite side, giving me a quizzical eye.

"Put this on so we can get you out of here," I ordered Baugi.

Baugi lifted the cylinder into the sunlight, recognizing it. "Oh," he said, "you drag Baugi out of here." He put on the belt with familiarity. "We used to play with these," he said and gave me a wink with his only eye.

The trees rustled in front of us. I scrambled to Hazi, grabbed one of the weapons she laid out, and aimed it in the direction of the sound of movement. Hazi propped herself up, training her bow and arrow toward the reptiles. A reptilian stepped into the open, crouched, and stretched his head upward. Hazi shot the arrow, piercing him through the throat.

Crackling sounds of gunshots burst from the brush. Reptilians hurried out, firing their weapons and taking cover behind nearby boulders. I ducked my head, taking cover behind the hill on which we positioned ourselves. Baugi pulled out the big gun, stood up in the open, and fired. He handled the weapon with ease as he kept it steady, spraying bullets across the field. He struck several reptilians, shredding their limbs. They fired back.

Hazi discharged her bow without exposing herself, but the enemy was able to evade her arrows. She grabbed a pulse pistol and shot it, striking one of our attackers in the eye, splattering the back of his head. Baugi grabbed me and lunged me toward Hazi. A grenade detonated nearby, but Baugi blocked the blast with his back, taking in shrapnel. The wounds did not faze him. He swung around with his gun and laid down a suppressing fire, forcing the pursuers to take cover again.

Hazi set up a weapon, affixed to a tripod, and fired a projectile vertically into the air. The projectile arced downward behind the enemy, exploding harmlessly. Frustrated at her poor aim, she grabbed another grenade and, without using the launcher, hurled it amidst our enemy. The grenade exploded on contact, shredding several reptilian bodies.

Within seconds, the reptilians resumed their fire with intensity, forcing us to take cover. I plugged my ears with my fingers, muffling them from the deafening noise, and tightened my eyes shut. When the shooting slowed down, I rolled over to see a large reptilian warcruiser above closing in.

"We can't hold them," Hazi yelled. "And if that warcruiser gets in range, we're done for."

Baugi lifted his gun and took aim but was knocked backward by a bullet that struck his shoulder.

"What's taking them so long?" I muttered, referring to Sargin and Malah.

I rolled to my right and spotted several reptilians leaping between rocks, trying to flank us. One of the reptilians raced out from the cover of one boulder, trying to reach the next one. I shot at him.

The slide on my gun locked back. I was out of ammunition, so I reached for another weapon. "A dragon would be good about now," I grumbled.

Hazi expended the ammunition from her weapons and threw them down after her last shot. With fluidity, she grabbed her spear and prepared for another wave of attacks. Baugi did the same, but with ammunition still available in his gun, he readied himself with both weapons. In his left hand was a spear, and in the right was the large gun.

We saw movement to our right. Baugi fired in that direction toward several reptilians, but they kept their heads down and continued their flanking.

"We aren't going to make it," I said.

"Stop being a pessimist," Hazi yelled, keeping an eye out for a target.

Bullets cracked overhead, and I dropped to the ground. The reptilians were getting closer, and their gunshots were growing louder.

"We need to do something," I yelled.

An explosion shook the ground. I covered my head from falling debris, then looked back to see smoke masking the side of the crashed aircraft. The two scout vehicles flew out from the craft and turned in our direction. Their weapons pulverized the boulders our aggressors used for cover, blasting the reptilians along with the rocks.

One of the vehicles pulled up next to us. Sargin opened the hatch. "Get in!" he yelled. I leaped into the back seat next to Andros.

Hazi jumped into the craft driven by Malah. Her spear was too long for the cabin, so she positioned it with the tip poking out the back window.

Sargin held up his remote control and activated it. Baugi fell forward uncontrollably and hovered over the ground, attached to an electric line connecting him to Malah's scout. Baugi quickly regained his senses, grasping his spear and gun. We throttled forward. I looked behind in time to see the reptilian warcruiser fire on our wrecked craft, blasting it to oblivion.

"Yes," Sargin cheered, proud of his escape. His celebration was short-lived, as his panel alarm sounded.

CHAPTER 20
EARLY MORNING

The massive reptilian warcruiser, which was nearly a half mile in length, launched infiltrators. They swarmed the skies, then formed into a group, speeding after us with guns blazing.

Sargin evaded the attacks with intricate maneuvers, but the vehicle was not designed to protect its occupants from constant jolts in every direction. Andros, being unconscious and unable to brace himself, hit his head several times. His body was flung like a roller-coaster rider, held in place only by a safety belt.

The third time the reptilian hit his head on the window, he grunted. The ridges on his head probably protected him from a concussion. Andros opened his eyes, looked at the window, and then bobbed his head toward me. "What's going on?" he asked sluggishly.

"We're being attacked!" I screamed, pointing at the attackers to our rear.

Andros twisted his body, assessing the situation for himself. "Oh, I see," he said, turning back around and stretching his arms forward. "Yeah. We're in trouble," he mumbled, then dropped his head, falling unconscious again.

"Did he just wake up and pass out again?" Sargin yelled with curt disdain.

"I'm trying to figure out how he's still alive," I yelled back.

"Me too," Sargin said, swerving, knocking Andros back into the window with a thud to his head. "He's lost a lot of blood, and brain cells for that matter."

"I'm not talking about that," I screamed. "I'm talking about your driving!" Sargin swerved the craft again, knocking my head into the window. "Someone didn't think things through when they designed this vehicle," I spat with sarcasm, pressing my palm against the part of my skull that hit the window.

"Normally we wear helmets," Sargin yelled back, taking another sharp turn.

"Where are they?" I asked, checking below my seat.

"In the storage box on the outside," he said.

I rolled my eyes. "Of course they are!"

"Would you like me to pull over so you can get one?" Sargin asked with rhetoric sarcasm.

"You know," I spat back. "I bet you've got some serious road rage problems, don't you?"

He didn't answer.

Racketing gunfire hit the craft on the side, and Sargin reflexively banked hard to the right, smacking my head back into the window. "For crying out loud! You're going to break whatever's in my skull," I fussed, holding my head and feeling a trickle of blood near my ear.

Malah's scout moved in closer to us, and I could see Baugi being dragged behind, floating and firing at the infiltrators. Malah banked to his left, and Baugi swerved to the side, giving me a clear look at his face. Baugi smiled, enjoying himself.

Baugi was flung to the other side as Malah swung right. Despite the whipping back and forth, Baugi enjoyed a much smoother ride than those of us inside the scouts. The devices he wore seemed to have some form of dampener that minimized the effect of acceleration on his body.

Sargin steered right, slamming my head into the window just in time to see bright blaster fire strike nearby. "Stop hitting my head!" I screamed, rubbing what I was convinced was going to be a large bump. "You are literally supposed to be protecting it," I whined, feeling like a bobblehead doll.

"Yeah, yeah," Sargin mocked. "I hear you. Now shut up!"

"You shut up!" I hollered back.

Pellets from a blast struck our windshield. Sargin throttled ahead at full speed. He was no longer swerving but found an open plain and sped forward as fast as he could. The reptilians sacrificed the accuracy of their firing for speed, but the shots still pelted our craft.

One of the blasts that hit the terrain below us knocked us upward. "What was that?" I yelled.

"A freaking big reptilian ship!" Sargin said.

Andros, with his head bouncing, mumbled to himself in a dream like state, "Chubby, chubby, chubby."

Turning back, I could see the warcruiser hovering above and moving forward, eclipsing the sun. Cannon fire erupted from the ship again, sending a barrage of projectiles toward us. They struck the ground around us, flinging dirt into the air.

Sargin's panel squawked. "We have a channel," he said, static roaring in the intercom overhead. He veered to the left and slapped a toggle switch. "This is Prince Sargin of Ganteep," he announced. "Reptilians are in pursuit of me and another scout vessel. We need assistance!" Static returned, but nobody answered his call for help. Sargin leaned forward, scanning the horizon. On his left side, he found something of interest and spun the steering wheel to make a hard turn in that direction.

My eyes bulged at the sight of the plain beneath us dropping down a steep mountainside. "Don't do it!" I yelled, icy fear rushing through my veins while I braced myself.

"Too late!" Sargin yelled back, just as terrified as I was.

Our speed launched us beyond the cliff, but gravity kicked in and plunged us downward. I gasped in horror at the ground speeding up toward us. Sargin and I screamed.

"Not smart," he yelled. "Bad idea," he chastised himself.

The vehicle vibrated and bounced against plants and shrubs on the mountainside.

"We're dead!" I screamed, feeling my brain smothered against the back of my skull.

Sargin was yelling in horror with a loud pitch.

We reached the bottom, skidding on the ground to a sudden stop with a loud crunch. Our safety straps kept our bodies in place, but some of the metal plating was crumpled near the front. The antigravity mechanism kicked in and brought us back to a hover. Sargin wasted no time in accelerating forward, shoving our heads into the headrests. The risky maneuver worked. Sargin opened the gap between us and our pursuers. Static on the intercom drained out all other sounds.

I looked back to see Malah still following us. Baugi held on to his spear with both hands. The gun was probably lost after that suicidal plunge.

Our hard-earned gap lasted only moments. Infiltrators fired upon us, hitting our engines and causing us to lose momentum.

"For crying out loud," Sargin screamed, stomping at the floorboard. Our vessel went dead, limping in midair, as the other engine gave out too.

Malah slung his vessel around to provide us with covering fire. Sargin worked frantically, flipping switches to restart our scout. One engine reactivated with a loud scream that deafened even the overhead static. We moved forward, but not nearly as fast. At this rate, the reptilians could pick us off in no time.

Sargin ran his fingers across the controls, trying to find anything that he could use to get us out of here, but he found nothing and slammed his fists on the dashboard.

The static ceased as the intercom clicked. "Scout vessel. We received your message. Stand by."

Then, in a blinding light, the warcruiser exploded above us, the shock wave streaking through the sky in all directions. Infiltrators tried to scurry away, but they were picked off by unknown assailants.

Sargin screamed out in victory. I looked ahead and saw jets dogfighting the infiltrators, defeating them at every point. Farther back were larger Ganteep aircrafts that looked like flying fortresses.

Within less than a minute, the skies were filled with smoke, and the ground with wreckage and flames. We were joined by scout vessels, similar to the ones we were in.

"This is General Pierre of Ganteep Outpost One," called a voice through the intercom. "We will be escorting you to base." I laughed in relief.

Sargin flipped the toggle switch. "Much appreciated, General," Sargin said, letting out a long breath.

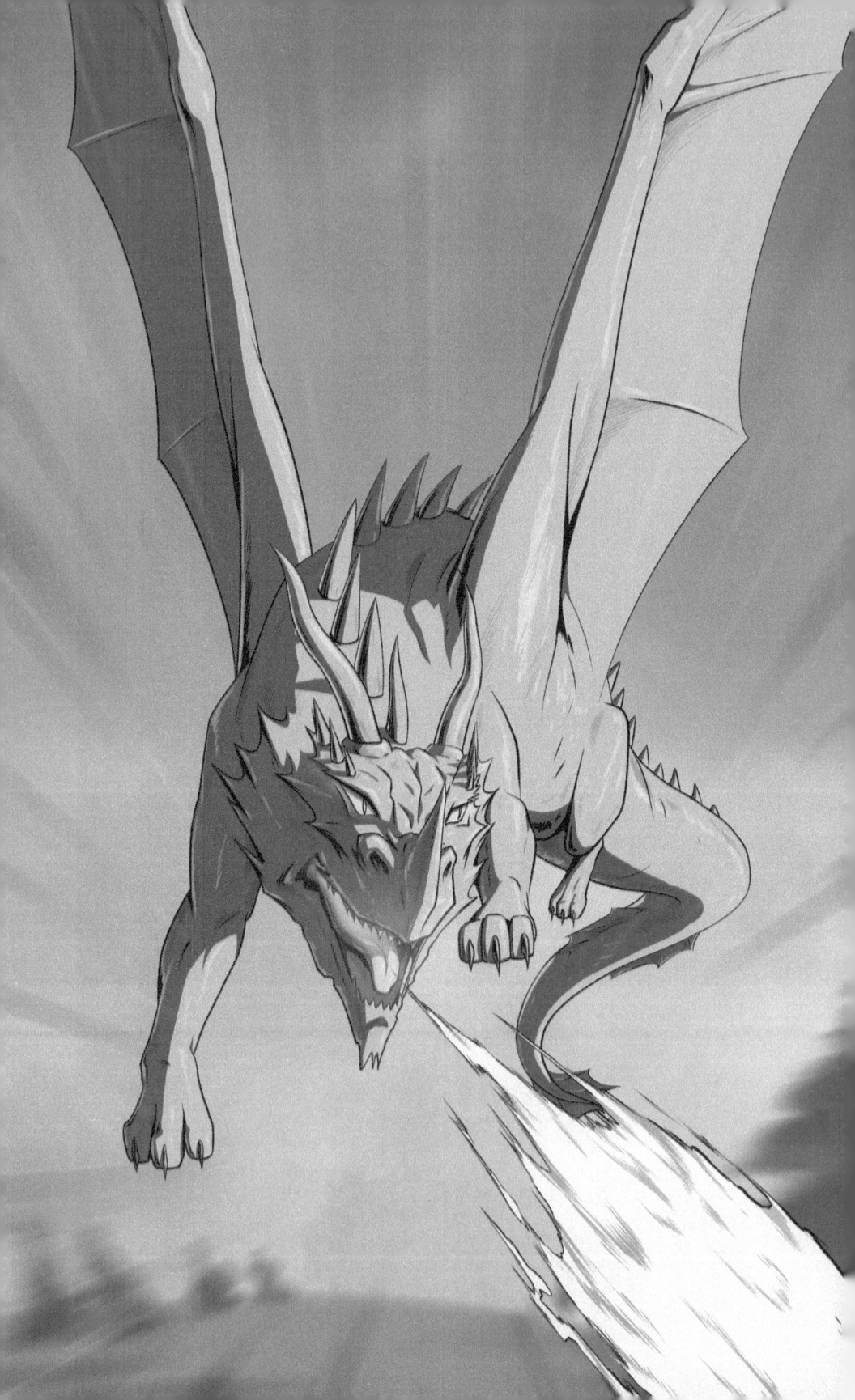

PART III

CHAPTER 21
MORNING

General Pierre shoved a finger at Andros. "Take him into custody," he ordered.

Two Ganteep soldiers lifted the hatch to our scout vessel. Andros, unconscious, fell into the arms of one of the soldiers. They repurposed the antigravity devices that Baugi wore, placed them on the reptilian, and pushed him away.

I sat on the ground with my head buried in my knees, trying to rid myself of a throbbing headache and dabbing at a head wound with a piece of cloth that a medic handed me.

"A little beat up there, eh?" General Pierre asked, standing over me, combing his hand through his white hair. Burn marks on his face caused his right eye to droop without an eyebrow.

"Yeah," I said without lifting my head. "It's going to be one heck of a headache."

"Next time, wear a helmet," the general suggested with mockery. Below my knees, out of sight, I extended my middle finger toward him. I heard the doctor snicker in the background.

Malah approached the general. "Enkidu," he began, but the general cut him short.

"Your dragon is safely with us," General Pierre confirmed.

Sargin lifted my head up gently by the chin, inspecting me for injuries. The general intertwined his fingers, waiting for Sargin to finish his inspection.

"This is Keiji, General," Sargin said. "He's a traveler."

"I'm assuming there is some relationship between Keiji's presence and the reptilian attack," Pierre speculated, frowning at me with suspicion.

"I think I'm here *because* of the attack," I suggested, attempting to correct the general's reasoning.

Pierre took Sargin to the side to speak privately.

A squad of soldiers talked excitedly about Baugi while Hazi tended to his wounds. Many had never been so close to a giant before, so the opportunity to meet a giant, despite the bad blood between the races, was a thrill. A few yards away, Malah regaled soldiers with tales about our escape from Ganteep City and the long night in the Land of Darmant.

Pierre waved me over. "Why don't we get you guys patched up, fed, and rested," he said. "How does that sound?"

"I'm not sure I can sleep," Sargin said, stuffing his hands deep into his pockets.

"We have some meds that can take care of that," Pierre assured.

***

My quarters were sparse but luxurious. Rugs with hexagonal patterns stretched across a concrete floor. Yellow sunlight shone through the copper-tinted windows, casting flowing shadows onto the walls.

My clothes were taken away for washing and repair. I was left with a nightgown, a robe, and slippers. Being filthy, I only put on the robe.

The bathroom walls were made of rocks mortared together, and at the far end was a small pool rippling as water flowed steadily from a fountain. I stood near the water and felt the heat from the steam, forcing my face to sweat.

I dipped my toe into the water. *Oh, so warm!* I dropped my robe and slid myself into the bath. My tense muscles eased. I inspected my bruised knee, then closed my eyes and felt my mind drift away.

A half hour later, I submerged under the water, scrubbed my face, and raked my hair back with my fingers. I lifted my head above the surface and opened my eyes. At the opposite end of the bath, various soaps of different sizes and shapes had been laid out. Two of the soaps caught my attention. The first was purple with ripples, and the other was a bar of green soap. I used them to bathe and massage my aching body. Once finished, I grabbed a towel and returned to my room.

A plate of hot food sat on a table by the bed, along with a glass of water. After dressing in the nightgown, I sat on the bed to eat. The platter hosted a combination of fish, eggs, and bread. I lifted the glass of water and saw no specks floating in it. Perfectly clear.

Once I consumed the food, I lay down and drifted to sleep.

I dreamt about walking in the park near my home. Birds flew above without any care, singing. The wind brushed across my face. I opened my eyes to a clear blue sky. The sun rose, and its rays warmed my body.

The sun grew brighter. The birds stopped singing and began a frantic chatter. The ground shook, and I looked up to see an angry moon staring back at me. Like a shell, it cracked, and blood poured out, racing to me in tides. I braced for impact.

I opened my eyes, dripping in sweat.

"Are you okay?" an unfamiliar voice asked.

I rolled over to see a young male medic tending to my wounds.

"How long did I sleep?" I asked, rubbing my eyes.

"A good part of the day," he answered, standing and circling to the end of my bed. "You will probably want these." He patted my folded clothes that replaced my food tray on the table. "They are clean, so why don't you get dressed. The general requested you to join him for dinner. By the way, if you want to clean your mouth, use the brush at the sink."

Leaning forward, I scratched the back of my scalp, averting the medic's gaze. When he turned away, I cupped my hand over my mouth, trying to smell my breath. *Yuck!*

He walked to the bathroom to wash his hands, leaving me alone to get dressed. My knee was bandaged and no longer hurt. I turned my back toward him while dressing, giving me some semblance of privacy. All the rips in my clothes had been patched or stitched back together. Once dressed, I brushed my teeth, and we left the room.

"You don't happen to know the whereabouts of a dragon, do you?" I asked the medic, who led me down a corridor.

"Enkidu?" he confirmed, so I nodded. "He's having his wounds tended to as well. I can't believe he was able to fly. He took a real beating."

"Will he be okay?" I asked, recalling the harrowing defense he and his sons made during our escape from Ganteep City.

"I think so," he said. "Come. I'll take you to see him."

The medic escorted me to an enormous atrium within the building and approached a railing set about four stories high. Below, Enkidu lay while caregivers rubbed ointments on his wounds. Large stitches closed a long gap on his back leg. The medical team resembled ants scurrying on and around the dragon.

Enkidu appeared to be napping while they worked on him. He stirred himself awake, quickly catching sight of us. Recognizing me, he rose as if in greeting. I reached out with my hand, and he stretched his neck, bringing his head close enough to let me stroke the side of his face.

He purred. A rush of excitement stood my hair on end. *I am petting a dragon!*

"Dragons are quite marvelous," the medic said.

"Oh yes," I murmured, still grinning. Enkidu lowered his head to the ground and rested.

"Unfortunately, he may be the last one," the medic informed me. "According to Malah, Enkidu had a mate who bore him three sons but died soon after their births," the soldier explained. "Malah said the three sons were killed trying to protect you while fleeing from Ganteep City."

"They did," I said, biting my upper lip as I recalled hearing Enkidu's screams in my head each time one fell. The sorrow and pain that he felt was still a haunting memory.

We left Enkidu and headed to the general's quarters. Once there, we entered a spacious dwelling with a sizable table in its center. Seated across from each other were Sargin and Malah. The medic bade me farewell, then took his leave.

"Where are Hazi and Baugi?" I asked, joining my two companions.

"They weren't interested in politics," Malah said, reaching out and choosing a piece of fruit from a bowl on the table. As if on cue to prove Malah wrong, both Hazi and the giant entered, followed by Pierre and his entourage.

Pierre crossed his arms, thumbing his jaw. "Scout ships just returned from Ganteep City," he said.

Sargin propped his elbow on the table, urging the general to continue.

"The capitol building was decimated," the general apprised the prince. "I have decided to declare your father dead."

Sargin gently dropped his head, trying not to show his emotions.

General Pierre relaxed his arms and let them drop to the side. "On behalf of the military, I'm officially recognizing you as king," he said, giving Sargin a small bow.

The new king never looked up but rather grabbed a utensil and tapped it on a plate. "I'm hungry," he said, trying to distract himself from being taken by grief. "Let's eat."

CHAPTER 22

AFTERNOON

The food on the table reflected the colors of the rainbow. The flawless purple grapes the size of golf balls, bright red and blue berries I didn't recognize, wedges of yellow and orange citrus, and a vibrant array of green vegetables whetted our appetites. I bit into a grape like it was a plum, but Baugi tossed one into his mouth whole and chewed. The sound of seeds crunching in his mouth reverberated across the dinner table. Hazi dove into her food using her hands, whereas Malah elegantly sliced into his steak using a two-pronged fork and a knife. The mashed potatoes were exquisite.

"Why didn't you help defend Ganteep City when it was attacked?" I asked General Pierre, not that I thought it would have made any difference.

"We don't abandon our posts," the general replied. He cut a slice of meat and took a bite. "This is our most distant post on the planet, outside of Ganteep City," he said while chewing. "We are bordering the Haran wilderness. Your little night escapade in the Land of Darmant is a cakewalk compared to a night in Haran."

"Haran?" I asked, spitting a grapeseed into my napkin.

The general placed his knife neatly at the top of his plate. "Haran is swarming with predators. I'm guessing she knows all about that," he said, slouching and arching his only remaining eyebrow at Hazi.

Hazi shifted her weight. "The wilderness of Haran is a place my people go for our trials. It's a rite of passage. When we are old enough, we enter the forest," she said, resting her elbows on the table. "Those who survive forty days and nights are rewarded with the status of the warrior class. Everyone else earns their position in our society based on the number of days they spend in the wilderness."

"And if they don't go into the Haran wilderness?" Malah asked, taking another bite.

"They are not allowed to rejoin our society," she answered. "Simply put, they are exiled. This has caused some problems because many of those outcasts have united and created alliances with other races. Giants included," she said, flashing an eye at Baugi, whose interest in the conversation had long since waned.

"Where are they now?" I asked, biting into my steak. The tenderness of the meat and the delectable flavor of spices made my mouth water between each bite.

"Dispersed into several colonies, but I've heard there is a thriving community at the other end of the Haran wilderness. I believe the place is called Untermeth," she said, reaching for a loaf of bread. "Rumor has it that they are very advanced technologically." She bit into the hunk of bread.

"Those rumors are true," Pierre confirmed, taking a gulp from his wine glass. "We used to keep an eye on those at Untermeth, but they proved to be a peaceful bunch, so we let them be." Pierre let out a chuckle. "Well, almost."

"What do you mean by that?" Malah asked.

Pierre set the glass on the table. "Let's just say they have their quirks. Our bigger concerns are north of Haran in the caves, not too far from Darmant. Do you know what happens there, young Keiji?"

I frowned, shaking my head.

"Baugi knows," the giant grumbled, sitting on the floor. "People go in. People take giants in. Only people come out."

"I don't understand," I admitted.

Sargin breathed in deeply. "Reptilians?"

"That's our suspicion," Pierre said. "Their attack was brewing right under our noses."

Hazi cleared her throat but said nothing. If I understood the situation correctly, Baugi, having seen where the giants were taken, must have connected the dots that this was the place of the so-called "preserve" that Hazi referenced.

Sargin poked at the potatoes on his plate with a utensil, then perked up suddenly. "The drugs the medic gave me worked great. Slept like a baby," he said, complimenting the general's earlier suggestion. "How about you, Keiji? Sleep okay?"

"Pretty good, but I had a strange dream about the moon," I answered.

"Which moon?" the general asked, leaning back and tucking his thumbs into his belt.

"Our moon," I replied. "In my time, we have a moon. Some of our scientists believed the moon was created at the same time as this planet. Others believed the moon was captured into the Earth's gravity. The idea that it may have been brought here intentionally is theory proposed only by some." I grabbed a wine glass. "It is a bit surreal to think that some of the craters on the moon that I have looked upon my whole life were in fact created by Admiral Radau's bombardment."

"Radau?" the general asked, turning to Sargin, clearly recognizing the name.

"Before the reptilians attacked," Sargin began, "Radau intercepted this so-called moon and investigated it. He determined that it was a threat after it destroyed one of our probes."

The general leaned forward, raising his eyebrow with interest. "We've been tracking that thing," he said. "It is moving fast. I've received several reports suggesting that the object is wreaking havoc on our planet."

My ears perked up. "What kind of havoc?" I asked, remembering that Radau had mentioned something similar before his destruction.

"Earthquakes for one," he said, tightening his lips, "and massive tsunamis. If this keeps up, this planet will witness global flooding."

Is this Noah's flood? I thought.

"No," the doctor said in my head. "That happens later."

I was about to respond, but the doors opened. A soldier entered, stepped to the general, and whispered into his ear.

"We'll be right there," the general said, waving the soldier away. "That dream of yours about the moon may not be a dream after all," he said, reaching for his napkin. He wiped his face, then tossed it on the table, implying the meal was over.

We followed him into a dark cemented passageway that was big enough for a small vehicle to traverse. Electric bulbs lined the ceiling, tied together with cables.

"Please elaborate on what's going on," Sargin requested, keeping pace with the general.

"Let's get to the command center, your highness. We'll learn more there," Pierre suggested, accelerating his walk into a jog.

Alarms blared, and red lights with rotating beacons flooded the hallway. General Pierre quickened to a full sprint. Hazi, with spear in hand, kept up with the general by extending her stride into a trot. Baugi trailed behind, letting his spear racket against the roof and walls.

We veered into a side corridor where soldiers crossed before us through intersecting pathways. The alarms rang louder as we closed in on our destination.

My stomach leaped when the floor shook, knocking me down along with Malah and Sargin. Everyone else managed to brace themselves against the walls. I wrapped my arms around my head, blocking it from falling debris. Sparks flew when a light fixture wiggled loose and crashed to the floor.

The shaking stopped, leaving us covered in dust and wafting away smoke. Pierre heaved me upward. "Not much time," he warned. "Hurry!"

We approached a metal-wire gate flanked by security.

The general called out to the guards. "Let them through," he said, referring to us. They obeyed the orders and opened the gates that led us into another bunker. We traversed a hallway to a dimly lit passageway with red blinking lights on the walls until we reached a locked door. Pierre punched in a code, opening the door.

We were greeted by a tall short-haired man in uniform. "What's going on, Colonel Coppens?" Pierre asked, coming to a halt, short of breath.

"The object we're tracking has slowed, preparing for orbit," Coppens replied. The colonel pressed buttons at a control panel, displaying the object on an overhead screen. "We'll have to destroy it."

"Do you recognize that thing?" Pierre asked me, not letting his attention stray from the image. "Is that your moon?"

"Yes," I confirmed.

Pierre tapped his thigh. "Trying to destroy it, then, will be a wasted effort. However, maybe there is something we can do," the general said, staring at me with steel eyes.

CHAPTER 23
LATE AFTERNOON

Blinking lights drew my attention to an empty workstation. I put my arms on the unoccupied chair and hunched over to study the monitor. White dots were climbing from the bottom of the screen to the top.

"What does this mean?" I asked nobody in particular.

Pierre peered over my shoulder. "Looks like an evacuation," he speculated.

The doors opened behind us, and the sound of boots scampering in caught our attention. Spinning around, we came face-to-face with a duty officer. "We received a report that a mothership and several warcruisers could be seen leaving the planet," he reported.

The general pinched his chin. "It appears the reptilians are evacuating," he said, returning his attention to the workstation and tapping the monitor. "According to this, thousands of ships are hurrying away. I wonder why."

The idea of reptilians evacuating the surface was welcoming, but then the picture of bodies cultivated for food flooded my brain, giving way to nausea.

"How many do you think they culled?" I asked Hazi.

Hazi took a deep breath. "Millions," she said, maintaining a blank expression. "I suspect the reptilians culled millions of people."

Pierre cleared his throat. "I'd have to agree with you, Hazi," he said.

A soldier handed Pierre a piece of paper. He read it, then excused himself.

Are you there? I thought, reaching out to the doctor.

"Of course," the doctor replied. He spoke with a sullen tone.

Is it true? Millions of people have been taken up to serve as food for the reptilians? I hoped the answer was no.

"There is no evidence to the contrary," he answered, almost coldly. "The end of the Second Age is the least understood of all the apocalypses," the doctor said. "All we know is that it was the result of a massive attack by reptilians. However, some of us are convinced that invisible hands are maneuvering events throughout the timeline."

I'm guessing you are hoping that I will find more than just the scroll.

"Obviously," the doctor admitted. "If we can get any additional details on our hidden enemy, then we may get the upper hand."

Still seems like a high risk to send me here. You said the damage would be minimal by sending me here, but what about the reptilian timeline? Aren't they supposed to survive this? Did I kill any of them prematurely?

"We minimized that risk with self-correcting time loops," the doctor assured.

Self-correcting time loops? I asked, storming away from the console, rubbing my temples.

Hazi, noticing my frustration, looked on with concern.

I heard the doctor take a deep breath. "Your timeline has been locked," he stated. "Under normal circumstances, the timelines aren't locked, allowing for time travel both forward and backward. With locked timelines, you can't travel backward because the timeline can't correct itself if you do something that will make your future self impossible to exist. There will be severe consequences."

"Grandfather effect," I confirmed out loud. "If I kill my grandfather before my father is conceived, then I can't exist, and that would be bad." Hazi's ears perked up.

"Bad? No. Catastrophic," the doctor corrected. "That kind of situation could lead to a paradox, destroying your timeline. To prevent this, we put you in a sort of bubble so that you can physically move into the past. We sent you to a time where most everybody will die soon, so you really can't do too much damage, but if you do, the bubble can correct the situation."

"So if I kill somebody who is meant to live ...," I began.

"There will be an immediate correction," the doctor finished. "It's like rewinding a tape."

"I haven't seen anything like that," I said.

"If it happened, you probably did not notice," the doctor speculated.

I thought about the horrors of the past twenty-four hours. Millions of people were killed. Possibly, millions more culled. Cities destroyed. Horrendous space battles. All of it was supposed to happen. I pressed my back against the wall and watched the activity around me. Everything I was watching had already happened, but this was not a recording. These people were living in the now, unaware of their fate that lay ahead.

"Doctor, won't there be a problem with the timeline if I take that scroll with me to the future?" I asked, struck with the revelation.

"The scroll is time locked," he said. "It's in a bubble like you."

"Is it from the future?" I asked.

The doctor hesitated with his answer. "Not exactly," he said, sighing deeply. "You need to focus on your current situation," he pointed out, indicating the conversation was over.

Hazi massaged her jawline. "Interesting conversation you were having there," she said, dropping her arm. "Is it our destiny to die soon?"

I shook my head. "I don't know," I moaned.

General Pierre returned to our party. "It's confirmed. All reptilian vessels that were on the surface have left and returned to their motherships."

"Why do I think there is more," Sargin blubbered.

"We have picked up a different class of ships with a design we are unfamiliar with," Pierre said. "They are entering our atmosphere." Pierre lowered his head and turned slowly to me. "Why you? Why now? I don't believe in coincidences."

Sargin ran his fingers along the edge of the workstation, then spoke up. "He's here for a Kantara Scroll. We must get to Midlatica."

Pierre tightened his lips. "Those scrolls are not exactly public knowledge," he whispered, browsing the room to ensure no eavesdroppers were listening in.

"Now is not the time to be secretive," Sargin objected to the general's concern. "Can you help?"

Pierre pulled out the chair from the workstation, took a seat, and patted his thighs. "Midlatica," the general mumbled in deep thought. "I can't get you there, but I can get you to Hazi's pals at Untermeth. That place might have something that can fly that far."

The ground shook, knocking Pierre's chair backward and sending him to the ground. The wall nearest me cracked, blasting dust into the air. Baugi leaped from the corner and pushed Hazi and me to the floor and hunched over us. Heavy debris fell from the ceiling onto his back.

We waited for the rumbling to stop, then looked around, assessing the situation. Pierre and Coppens hurried to a workstation and conversed with the operator. The colonel slapped the back of the operator's chair, then turned his attention to us. "That earthquake was caused by your moon," he said, pointing a finger at me. "I wonder if we could destroy it."

"How are we supposed to do that?" Sargin huffed. "Radau fired everything he had at that thing, and nothing happened to it." Sargin was referring to the events that unfolded with the moon prior to engaging with a vast reptilian fleet.

"Something happened," Pierre corrected, knowing the moon's destruction was not an option. "We just don't know what."

"There was a great deal of anxiety when Radau used a nuclear weapon to destroy those reptilians," I interjected. "Why would that be?"

Pierre blinked a few times. "Nuclear weapons can rip the fabric of space. That's why they are outlawed. Radau was a levelheaded man. If he used it, then he had no other choice."

I scrunched my face in confusion. "Why have them then?" I asked. "Why have nukes in the first place?"

"A couple of reasons," Pierre said, raising two fingers. "The first is clearly for destructive purposes, which could have been Radau's intention, but I doubt it."

The general breathed in, not ready to divulge the second reason yet, but Malah stepped forward, eyes trained on him. "What's the other reason?" Malah asked.

The general contemplated the delivery of his answer, pushing his tongue into his cheek. "To send a message," he blurted. The group went silent until Baugi spoke.

"That's him," Baugi barked.

"Who?" I asked turning back.

"That's the one who saved me from the plane," Baugi answered, pointing to a screen on the wall.

I turned to see who Baugi was referring to, and my eyes widened with shock. Shivers traveled up my spine. "That's my father," I said with disbelief, recognizing my father's unmistakable gray eyes immediately.

The general corrected me. "That's Admiral Radau."

CHAPTER 24
NEARING DUSK

Alarms erupted with a loud screech. Thoughts about my father quickly dissipated. Pierre turned to the colonel. "What's happening?"

"Those ships we picked up are headed directly to us," Colonel Coppens answered. "Based on our scans, they are moving without the use of a propulsion system."

"A bit advanced for reptilians," the general pointed out.

Sargin scratched his head. "Then those ships belong to someone else."

"If that is the case, then the reptilians weren't acting alone." Pierre arched his eyebrow. "I think our true enemy is invisible."

"If only we knew who this enemy was," Sargin wished, "and why this allegiance with the reptilians?"

"Why not ask one?" I suggested.

Sargin and the general looked confused, but Baugi, who understood my suggestion, bellowed with amusement.

Malah gave a side panel a short jab. "Of course," he said. "Andros!"

***

The door slid open, and we entered a medical bay within the bunker. Beds lined the walls where whiteboards were hung with various scribblings. Patients, most of whom suffered from burns or broken limbs, occupied the beds while medics tended to them. Soldiers were cleaning the debris that had fallen from the preceding quakes. The automatic door whooshed shut behind us.

The colonel escorted us to a bed at the far end of the room where Andros lay unconscious with his wound exposed. The reptilian was covered only with a pair of oversized shorts. The rest of his clothes had been cleaned and were folded neatly on a table nearby. A blue field of light emitted from the ceiling to the floor, encapsulating the reptilian.

A tall, lanky man with white hair diverted his attention from Andros to us. He held an electronic tablet in his hands. I assumed the tablet was a patient chart.

"Checking in on the reptilian?" the man verified, tapping the edge of the tablet with his index finger. A large scar on the left side of his face stretched into his hairline, cutting off the tip of his ear.

"Yes, Doctor," Pierre said. "How is he?"

"We replicated his blood cells to replenish his loss of blood, treated the stab wound, and are monitoring his concussion," he said, pointing to the various parts of the reptilian's body as he spoke. "Resilient creature. He's going to recover just fine."

"I want to ask him some questions," Pierre stated, not worried about the impact that waking Andros up could have on his recovery.

The doctor frowned, narrowing his eyes. "Why? Have you learned to speak the creature's language?"

"Please, Doctor," I begged. "This is important."

The doctor's eyes bulged with astonishment at my words. He slid an instrument from his belt, flicked a switch upward, and then scanned me. "That's different." He rubbed the scar in his hairline. His easygoing nature during this time of chaos may have been the result of whatever he endured that caused the scar. He was cool under pressure.

Hazi rolled her eyes. "You didn't notice his clothes were out of place?" she hissed with sarcasm.

"I noticed your clothes," the doctor shot back, "or lack of them."

"Ha," laughed Baugi, pointing to the doctor. "Doctor funny."

Hazi huffed at the remark.

The doctor shifted his eyes toward me, then grinned. "You are indeed a great curiosity!"

"Yeah, yeah," Malah interjected. "Do you mind, Doctor?"

"Of course," the doctor answered, giving a curt bow and then entering the blue field. He pulled out a hypodermic syringe, injected something into the reptilian's shoulder, and then backed out of the field. "It will take a few moments for the drug to work."

Lifting his shirtsleeve to scratch his forearm, the doctor revealed his very own Midlatican bracelet. *Of course. He can move easily through the field because of his bracelet. What about Andros? He has a bracelet too.*

I tilted my head to get a better view of the reptilian's wrist, but the bracelet had been removed. I checked the area around me and found the bracelet on a table near the head of the bed, against the wall.

Andros moaned, yawned, then cracked his eyes open into small slits. He stretched his arms, then placed his hands on the area where he had been wounded. Satisfied that the wound was healing, the reptilian lifted himself up and leaned forward. He rolled his shoulders, giving a sigh of relief.

"My compliments to my healer," he hissed, eyeing the doctor with suspicion.

"Of course," the doctor said with an uncontrollable smile. He turned back to us. "I'm talking to a reptilian," he said, unable to hide the giddiness in his voice.

The general was less amused. "This reptilian partook in genocide, Doctor," Pierre informed him. "Let's tone down the enthusiasm."

Andros redirected his attention to the force field, then tapped it with his hand. He pulled his arm back quickly when the shield gave him a sudden static shock. "I see," he said, shaking out his hand. "I guess we still have some trust issues."

"You think?" the colonel spat out.

Pierre waved his hand at Coppens, silencing him, then directed his attention to Andros. "Did the reptilians act alone in this attack?" Pierre asked, getting right to the point.

Andros shifted his head to the left but maintained eye contact. "I don't think so," he admitted. The anger and curtness Andros showed earlier was gone. His facial expressions were less alien and more human. I assumed the doctor's intervention by accelerating Andros's brain was nearing completion.

"Explain," Pierre insisted.

Andros gripped the edge of the bed, then loosened his grip. "We may have superiority in numbers, but to mount an attack on the Ganteep home world could not possibly be done by just us. There is just no way. One of your battlecarriers would have easily obliterated our fleet. Let's face it: those are the ultimate war machines." He twitched.

"Why attack?" Pierre asked.

"Food shortages." Andros hopped off the bed, checked his balance, and paced within the field.

"Your people were hungry, then?" I confirmed. The image of my father entered my mind, but I swept it away to maintain my focus.

"Yes," he answered.

"Why are you cooperating with us now?" Pierre asked.

"I don't see you as food anymore. I think something happened when Keiji touched my head," Andros speculated. "Human meat isn't as appetizing as it once was." Andros halted and crinkled the skin on his forehead.

"Is that why you are so forthcoming?" the colonel asked.

"There is no place in my society for a passive, civilized reptilian," Andros said.

Sargin tilted his head over his shoulder, eyeing me. "What do you think, Keiji?" he asked.

I closed my eyes, searching for feelings emanating from Andros. He was like an open book. In fact, he seemed to be the only person in the immediate area emanating no deceptive thoughts. "He believes what he says," I confirmed. "I sense no deception on the part of Andros, unlike the general and the colonel."

Malah slapped his hand over his mouth, covering his smile. The colonel scowled with a vein bulging from his forehead. The general worked his jaw back and forth, caught in deep thought about what an appropriate response should be, but settled with a sigh.

"I think I found what I was looking for," Pierre said, slapping my shoulder. "Somebody else is consorting with the reptilians. Let's go."

"Hold on," I said, turning to Andros. "What is the plan? Why not just let the moon destroy us?"

"Diversion," Andros said. "The reptilian attack was only a diversion."

Sargin sighed. "All this for just food? There must be something more."

"I wouldn't know." Andros stopped abruptly, balancing himself by bracing his arm against the bed. "I don't think we knew about this base," he said, with revelation. "I'm guessing that my people know about it now."

"I think your guess is an accurate one," Pierre said. "We are picking up some ships returning this way."

Sargin raised his hand and stepped forward. "Why an egg?" he asked, referring to the moon.

Andros tightened his mouth. "I assume somebody intends to stay here for a very long time."

We huddled together so Andros could not hear us. "The scroll," Sargin said in contemplation. "What if our invisible foe is mainly interested in attaining the scroll?"

"That's a big leap to make," Pierre said, shaking his finger. "A lot of assumptions come with that theory."

"Maybe," Sargin replied, allowing his voice to trail off, tapping his chin with his fist. "Whatever the case, my father believed in the importance of that scroll, so our priority has to be retrieving it."

Pierre bit his lower lip. "Then let's get a plane loaded for Untermeth!"

CHAPTER 25
DUSK

Andros dressed and joined us in our walk to the flight line. His arms were free of the cuffs, and despite Colonel Coppens's objections, his weaponry was returned to him. It might not have been logical to trust a reptilian, but Andros was different. Logic did not seem to apply anymore. We knew he was not our enemy.

We crossed the flight line to our destination. Andros blinked, staring in awe at the large plane before him.

"You look impressed," I said to the reptilian. He didn't answer, so I trailed off, thinking out loud. "We have planes in my day."

Andros said, "I never took the time to appreciate what it takes to build something like this." He placed a hand on the side of the craft, taking in a moment to marvel at such an engineering achievement for the first time in his life.

Hazi noticed something more. "The sky is full of clouds," she said.

Dark clouds rolled above, blocking any residual light from the setting sun. The wind around us picked up, flapping my jacket.

We entered the craft. I heard the grumble of a dragon from within the cargo bay. I climbed a set of metal stairs to a platform.

Grasping the handles, I watched Malah coaxing Enkidu by petting him. The dragon's head was pointed to the rear of the craft where the cargo door remained open. Enkidu fit comfortably below.

Airmen busied themselves inspecting the plane while others across the airfield scurried to prepare their fighter jets for the upcoming battle.

I scampered down the staircase to join Malah. "Why doesn't he just fly?" I asked him.

"We are letting him rest his injured wing," Malah said. "But if he has to, he can fly."

Baugi and Hazi joined us, each with a spear in hand. Malah patted the dragon one last time, and then we joined our companions and headed to the passenger cabin. That is, all but Baugi, who remained with the dragon.

In the cabin, Andros fidgeted for a moment, then found a place to sit alongside various soldiers and airmen, who in turn tried to hide their trepidation of sitting so close to a reptilian.

"Here we go again," I said, hoping this would not end in a crash landing.

Pierre entered the cabin with the colonel and several soldiers. "This is where we part ways," he announced.

Sargin hopped out of his seat, then grasped the general's hand. "I'm not sure what you can do here. Why don't you come with us?" Sargin suggested. "We could use your skills."

"I will never abandon my post," the general said, giving Sargin a firm handshake. "That is my duty to the king." The general left the cabin, leaving the colonel and the soldiers behind.

"The general ordered that I help you," Colonel Coppens explained.

"Please take a seat," Sargin insisted.

The colonel fell to the floor, rocketed by an unexpected earthquake. The overhead storage bins dropped open, emptying their contents.

The quake didn't cease, so the colonel braced himself and directed his attention to the pilot. "Get us out of here!" he ordered, then took a seat that pointed to the rear of the craft, much in the same way Enkidu lay in the cargo bay.

I was jolted forward with the sudden push by the plane. Outside, I watched a radar tower collapse where we were parked only moments before.

The pilot taxied to the runway and accelerated for takeoff. Through the outside windows, I watched jet fighters thrusting into the air, escorting us while we gained altitude.

"What is that?" Hazi pointed out a window to two large rectangular black ships hovering over Outpost One about a mile above the surface.

Andros unbuckled himself and pressed his face against a window. "Those are not reptilian ships," he confirmed, giving off an emotion of bewilderment.

The outpost fired ineffectively at the two ships while fighter jets attacked. Seconds later, the black ships dropped projectiles onto the outpost, obliterating it.

I felt like someone punched me in the gut. The colonel, who had unstrapped himself, straddled two seats with his arms and dropped his head in mourning. I didn't need him to say it. His feelings were focused on the general, who now was most certainly dead, much the same way King Sar died.

The mysterious ships pursued us, increasing their speed, and began closing the gap steadily.

The plane shuddered violently. At first, I thought it was turbulence, but the familiar sound of alarms wailed throughout the craft, alerting us of an attack. I clambered back up to my feet and rushed to the left window to assess the situation. Our escort was missing, and our engine was in flames.

I crossed over to the right side in time to see a jet explode. Our plane banked right. Bright white lights from outside flooded our cabin, followed by a loud thump, and our plane began to tremble.

I ran to the cockpit. "We're hit, aren't we?" I screamed.

Sargin gave me a disdainful look. "Get yourself strapped in," he yelled. I followed his orders by taking a seat in the chair directly behind him.

"This bird is going down," the pilot said.

"Maybe we can escape using the dragon. Are we low enough to breathe if we open the doors?" Malah asked.

"Yes," the pilot answered. "I'll try to keep her steady as long as I can!"

"Come with me," Malah urged.

We followed Malah down the stairs into the cargo hold, where he opened a panel and grabbed some ropes. Enkidu widened his eyes at the ropes. Realizing what Malah was up to, the dragon stretched forward, making it easy to wrap the ropes around his neck. Baugi helped by tying knots nobody could possibly unravel. He finished creating his makeshift harness and saddle. Malah climbed onto Enkidu and waved for us to follow.

Hazi leaped onto the dragon's back and held on much the same way Malah did. I slipped, but Baugi grabbed my shirt and hoisted me onto the dragon's back. The colonel and his soldiers hopped on. Then Baugi crawled onto the dragon's back, forcing Enkidu to grunt.

"This is nuts!" I screamed.

"Come on!" Sargin yelled at the cockpit, wanting them to join us, but nobody answered.

"If they leave their post, the plane will spiral out of control," the colonel barked at Sargin.

Frustrated, Sargin clenched his teeth together, giving Malah a nod. Malah slid off the dragon's back and slapped a red panel. The plane jerked, slamming Malah into the wall.

The cargo ramp dropped, and the cool air flooded in. Enkidu leaned his body toward Malah so that he could grab a rope. The sudden movement surprised me, and I gripped harder and braced myself with my feet, fearing I might fall off the dragon.

Enkidu rolled upright, bringing Malah up as he did so. "Hold on!" Malah yelled.

The rectangular ships were close enough for me to see through the windows where crew members passed by glowing walls. Two of the figures stood motionless in the centermost window, watching us. Enkidu lifted and thrust himself out the back of the plane, diving toward the surface of the planet.

A beam cracked through the air above and struck our plane like lightning, disintegrating it.

I felt Enkidu's muscles tense as he shot like a meteorite toward the ground. I pressed my body flat onto his scales, allowing the air to blow harmlessly above me. The wind softened as Enkidu slowed. He spread his wings, bringing us to a smooth glide above the surface, then made a soft landing.

My hands eased up, and I breathed a sigh of relief.

One of the soldiers fell clumsily to the ground, and Malah turned on a flashlight, shining it on him. "I'm okay," the soldier assured, extending his thumb to let us know all was well.

Enkidu snapped his head with alarm and, without preemption, spread his wings and leaped into the air, grunting under the weight of the giant.

Below, the soldier hollered for us to return, but his holler increased in pitch to a scream. Malah's flashlight gave us a glimpse of an animal leaping onto the soldier.

My eyes bulged in recognition of the attacking beast. "Was that a dinosaur?"

CHAPTER 26
EVENING

Enkidu soared through the air with elegance and swiftness. The image of the soldier attacked by a dinosaur-like creature ingrained itself in my mind. To redirect my thoughts, I twisted my head to look over my shoulder to verify the ships were indeed falling farther behind. Whatever their interests were, they did not bother pursuing Enkidu.

Who were they? What role did they play in this attack?

Loosening my grip, I gave myself permission to relax. One could only speculate as to whom the reptilians had collaborated with. What wasn't speculative was that Andros was unfamiliar with the technology of the ships that attacked the outpost.

Perhaps the mystery the doctor sought originated with those ships.

Enkidu's muscles flexed, catching me off guard. I tightened my hold on the ropes. Enkidu flapped his wings to gain altitude, then eased back into a glide. I returned my attention to our rear, where I watched the mystery ships rise in altitude. With a flash, both ships shot away and disappeared. All that was left was the fiery remains of their attack, which lit up the evening sky.

Amidst the bright backdrop of the orange embers of Outpost One, a large head rose above the trees, using its mouth to scrape the leaves off the branches. There was no mistaking what I was seeing. It was a dinosaur, at least the way I'd pictured they would look when I was in grade school. I tried to put a name to the dinosaur. *Brontosaurus? Brachiosaur? Something else?* I guessed the beast was hungry for an evening snack.

I thought dinosaurs have been extinct for millions of years. I wondered, hoping the doctor was listening.

"Were you there?" the doctor asked sarcastically, not expecting an answer. "The past holds many secrets. Much of what you think you know is wrong."

Wrong, eh? I thought to myself, with my attention diverted to the parting clouds in the sky, revealing a bright-white moon shining on us. This was a sight I was accustomed to, but this was different. This was the first time the moon dominated the evening sky. My companions also looked upon the moon, but to them, it was the sign of an ending. To me, the moon gave me a small sense of belonging to the planet again.

Enkidu descended onto a plateau that overlooked a jungle beneath us. He was in desperate need of a rest. I slid off the dragon, grateful to stretch and rest my arms and hands, but then a sudden thought of attacking dinosaurs crept into my mind, and I wanted to return to the safety of Enkidu's back. Everyone around me probably had similar thoughts because they wasted no time pulling out their weapons.

"This land is full of dinosaurs," I said to Hazi. "You trekked these forests?"

Hazi pulled off her equipment, inspecting it. "A good test for a warrior, don't you think?"

"If you don't die," I said, shaking my pistol.

"It happens a lot," she said, jabbing her spear into the ground. "Can't say I'm looking forward to being back."

"How far into this forest did you go?" I asked.

"Not this far," she answered.

"What attacked the soldier when Enkidu landed the first time?" I asked her.

"A feroxraptor," she answered, biting her lips. "They are pack hunters, so the one we saw was most likely not alone."

Hazi quickly scouted the area for any signs of danger to our party. She found none and suggested we build a fire. The colonel agreed. With the frigid air rolling in, we were happy for warmth, and Enkidu obliged by lighting the wood. With a fire-spouting dragon around, there was no need for the lighter in my pocket.

Enkidu wrapped his tail around his body and dozed off. Hazi and I took first watch while the others slept.

"I've never heard of a feroxraptor," I said, remembering names such as the velociraptor.

"When we perform our rite of passage, we must trek into a valley where a tree sprouts golden leaves," she said. "If we brought back one of these leaves, we accomplished our goal. It is about three weeks by foot to reach it and three weeks back, hence the forty days. About a half century ago, reports of feroxraptors nesting near the tree erupted. Several died in the attempt to capture a golden leaf, so our trials were limited to only surviving the forty days." Hazi pulled up some grass with her fingers, then pitched it forward.

"Has anyone been able to bring back a leaf since those raptors showed up?" I asked.

"Only one," she said with a grin, "and you're sitting next to her."

"I'm not surprised," I said, rocking my head back and forth.

"It came at a price though" she said, resting her elbow on her knee. "I was undergoing trials with my twin brother. I created a diversion for him, and he grabbed his leaf, but when he returned the favor, he was flanked by raptors. I got my leaf, but I lost my brother." She stretched her arms. "The journey back was the longest of my life."

We sat in silence, letting her story sink in. "Why didn't he just grab both leaves at the same time?" I asked.

"Respect for the tree does not allow it. Only one per person," she said.

"Where is the leaf?" I asked.

"Molded in the spearhead," she said, pointing to it. "It's the reason this weapon has such strength."

Picturing a leaf molded into a spearhead was difficult to imagine. Then again, Hazi used it to gouge Baugi's eye, and it was the same one used to crush through the window of an infiltrator. "Sounds like that's an invaluable spear," I said.

I stepped closer to the fire, warming my hands. A soldier slept nearby, peacefully, while another kept tossing, unable to find a comfortable position. I felt no empathy toward them. I didn't even want to know their names. I did not want to get attached to people that were likely going to die within the next day. No need to create any unnecessary attachments and subject myself to extraneous emotional turmoil.

CHAPTER 27
DAWN OF THE FIFTH DAY

The cool morning dew made my skin feel clammy. To loosen my body from the aches and pains of the previous few days, I jogged in place, then warmed my hands over the campfire, which was kept lit throughout the night. Movement in the corner of my eye caught my attention. Two soldiers stepped dangerously close to the end of the plateau behind some shrubs. My skin crawled with anxiety, expecting a feroxraptor to jump out and devour them.

"Are they fools?" I asked, pointing at them.

"Gotta take care of business," the colonel said. "Don't worry about them." A minute passed, and the soldiers returned unharmed.

Then the dragon rose and took flight. I watched him fly into the clouds and disappear.

"Needs to stretch his wings," Malah said, joining me by the fire, "and get something to eat. We'll have to travel the rest of the way on foot. Don't worry. Enkidu will be able to find us when he's ready."

My stomach dropped at the idea. "What about those dinosaurs? Those feroxraptors? I'd feel more comfortable if he was nearby."

"Can't be helped," Malah said, strapping his gun belt to his waist. "Besides, Baugi is just a bit too big for the dragon."

Colonel Coppens directed the soldiers to put the campfire out, then brought Sargin a slice of bread.

"How far is Untermeth?" Sargin asked the colonel.

Coppens pointed to the far end of the plateau. "Not far really," he said.

Baugi woke up with a loud snort. He sat up, rubbing sleep from his eye.

"Sleep well?" the colonel asked him.

The oversized man ignored the question.

Baugi reminded me of tales about giant one-eyed creatures known as cyclopes. "Baugi, can I call you Cy?" I couldn't help myself.

The giant rolled his eye, giving me a look of disdain. "I'm not a cyclops," he said. "That's a different clan."

Malah, who had been helping the soldiers kick dirt onto the campfire, joined the conversation. "It doesn't hurt to have a well-rested giant by our side if we are going to hike through a dinosaur-infested forest, so don't pick on him," he cautioned me.

"Sorry," I said, dropping my head, trying to hide my grin. *How can you resist making a joke about a one-eyed giant?*

Hazi grabbed her gear. She made plans with the colonel, then took point, leading us into the forest. Baugi took the rear while the soldiers marched along our flanks.

About midday, Hazi halted, holding up her hand for us to do the same. She launched an arrow, and instantly, the brush ahead began to rustle frantically. She grabbed her ax and swung downward, then waved us forward. In the place where she swung her ax lay a twenty-foot-long decapitated snake. I was grossed out by the writhing of the snake's body while the eyes of the cold-blooded creature followed us.

I couldn't help but try to get a closer look, but Coppens gripped my shoulder. "Careful," he warned. "It's still alive, at least for now."

We heard a rumbling in the air, then spotted jets flying overhead. They were reminiscent of the Ganteep fighter planes.

"I guess we are heading in the right direction," Malah said, wiping the sweat off his brow.

One of our soldiers fired his rifle into the trees and quickly turned to run, but he tripped and fell on the decapitated snake. The disembodied head clamped onto the soldier's hand, causing him to jump up screaming. Malah pulled out a knife to help the soldier but was knocked away when a feroxraptor jumped out into the open and leaped onto the snake-bitten man, driving its talons into his chest. The dinosaur hissed at us, guarding its kill. Its body was gray, decorated with black stripes. Three horns protruded from the skull, and a row of spikes lined its back. The raptor snatched the dead body with its teeth and dragged him away while we fired our guns at it.

More raptors jumped into view. A pack. One leaped toward Hazi, but she swung her ax across the raptor's face, sending it squealing and kicking to the ground.

Baugi took his spear and bludgeoned a raptor with a single blow.

I watched in horror while a soldier was dragged off screaming, his legs in the mouth of a raptor. When the soldier was out of view, bones snapped, and the screams turned to a gurgle.

One of the raptors stopped, coming face-to-face with Andros. The reptilian waved his hand at the dinosaur, and it followed, giving us hope for a fate other than becoming a dino-lunch. "Who's your daddy?" Andros joked, but the raptor lunged at him, and Andros turned, running. "I'm not your daddy!" he screamed while the raptor gave him chase. Two other raptors followed while Andros shouted expletives. "Get them off!"

A piercing shriek erupted above as Enkidu darted down with fire bursting from his mouth, enveloping Andros's pursuers in flames. The burning raptors ran away, igniting the dry leaves below them.

A raptor stepped out into the clearing with its eyes set on me, crouching for an attack. Before he could act, Hazi lodged an arrow through its skull.

Enkidu landed, knocking a tree over with a deafening crack, and glowered at the remaining predators within the pack. The raptors lowered their heads, chirping in submission.

"What's going on?" I asked.

"It appears Enkidu is the alpha male," Malah said like a proud papa, slapping my back. "That's my boy!"

Chapter 28
EARLY MORNING

Andros rubbed the ridges on his head, eyeing the horned feroxraptors lying peaceably around. "One moment they are attacking us, and the next, they are sitting around like pets," he blurted.

"Pets? Well, don't go petting one though," Hazi warned.

Malah whispered to Enkidu, who then nodded in response. The dragon lowered his head, and Malah climbed on his back, untying the makeshift harness that served as our lifelines in the escape from our crashing airplane.

"I'm surprised he let us put that rope on him," I said to Malah, referring to Enkidu's willingness to be harnessed for the flight. "I thought they couldn't be domesticated."

Malah pulled out a dagger and cut several ropes, allowing them to drop off the dragon. "Enkidu isn't domesticated. He's intelligent, and he cares about us." Malah put his blade away. "Enkidu is a friend. Remember that."

I tapped Sargin's shoulder, who was watching Malah act playfully with the dragon. "What's their story?" I asked.

Sargin stroked the stubble on his face. "Their story goes back a couple of centuries," he began, reminding me I was but a babe amidst the group. Malah could easily be more than five hundred years old. "Malah saved Enkidu's life."

"How?" I asked, turning my attention back to the captain.

Sargin slapped my shoulder. "That's a tale for another time," he said, dropping his hand and letting his voice trail off, "if we get out of this mess." Sargin shifted, then continued. "Anyway, Enkidu has been loyal to Malah ever since, hence why my father promoted him to captain of his guard."

"Because Malah controlled the dragon?" I asked.

Sargin shook his head. "No. He doesn't control Enkidu at all." He grabbed a pebble from the ground and flicked it away. "A dragon never gives loyalty to somebody who's unworthy, so it is rare when it happens. If someone is worthy of a dragon's loyalty, then, according to my father, that person is worthy of much more."

Enkidu stood up, creating a stir. The feroxraptors moaned and chirped, then scooted backward, giving Enkidu room to extend his wings. Enkidu flapped into the air and, once again, took flight.

"Where's he going?" Sargin asked.

Malah took a seat by Sargin, watching the dragon shrink in size the farther he flew away. "Probably scouting ahead," Malah speculated. "I can't be sure. It's not like Enkidu talks to me." Malah shrugged his shoulders.

The feroxraptors rose to their feet, then trotted in the same direction Enkidu flew, leaving us alone.

"I guess that's a sign. Let's move out," the colonel said, standing beside the only two soldiers who survived thus far.

We trudged through the forest for several hours without incident. The clouds parted for a while, and we took an open path where the sun beat down and warmed us.

The warmth of the sun was short-lived as the clouds closed again and cool wind rustled through the trees. The smell of decomposing leaves filled the air along with the occasional floral scent of wildflowers in nearby meadows. A gray squirrel scurried up a tree trunk, sending a small flock of birds into the sky. I kicked up dead pine needles throughout my hike. The temporary peace made me forget the horrors of the war.

Behind me, Baugi rubbed his skull. The bandage around his missing eye was dirty and stained. I worried that his eye socket may get infected from our travels.

Hazi stopped abruptly, waving her hand downward. The soldiers took a kneeling stance while the colonel squatted beside her. Gunfire thundered, snapping the colonel's head back, knocking his body to the ground.

Without thinking, I dove, seeking cover while gunfire rained upon us.

"Ambush!" yelled Sargin.

I grabbed my pistol and aimed it in the direction of the attack. I was shoved forward from a soldier sprinting to the colonel's aid.

Hazi unleashed a storm of arrows into the brush. Screams followed. One of our soldiers lobbed a grenade in the direction of the screams. Men with ragged coats and armed with guns burst out of the brush and hurried away from the exploding grenade.

Once the blast settled, they began shooting at us again. Their faces were covered with black soot. We fired back, killing at least two of them.

We took cover behind some boulders and trees. The abundance of gunpowder in the air caused my eyes to water.

"How many?" Malah screamed.

"Don't know," said the soldier next to Hazi. "I'd guess at least a dozen or more." He rose to fire at our attackers but caught a round in the chest, dying instantly.

A grenade was lobbed at us, and we scampered backward, but with little time to find protection, the last of our soldiers fell on top of the grenade, dismembering his body but saving our lives.

"We can't keep this up," Malah yelled, holding his hands above his head while bullets ricocheted around him.

A familiar chirping sound erupted. Behind us, a pack of feroxraptors scrambled to our rescue. With biting and thrashing, they mutilated our enemy amidst their horrific cries of unmerciful pain.

The screaming waned, and all that could be heard was the chomping of flesh by the pack of feroxraptors enjoying their breakfast. Their presence was fortuitous, and thanks to our dragon.

Not our dragon.

The dragon.

I scanned for Enkidu in the cloudy skies, but he was nowhere to be seen.

Eventually, we continued our hike through the forest until we reached a river. We crossed it easily with Baugi's help, but the feroxraptors had no interest in getting their feet wet. Thus, we parted from our newfound allies.

CHAPTER 29
MORNING

Our journey led us to the home of our attackers, Untermeth. Under the forest's concealment and in a prone position, Sargin and I peered through our scopes and observed the movement of the local population entering and exiting through the gates of Untermeth, a city encircled with protective walls. A squad of soldiers huddled in front of the gates. They wore the same ragged coats as our attackers from across the river, their faces also covered with black soot. One man held his hand to his ear, attempting to listen with a receiver.

"What are they doing?" I asked.

"I'm not sure, but it may have something to do with the attack on us earlier," Sargin speculated.

"Reminds me of the reaction by the reptilians when the doctor activated our bracelets," I suggested.

Sargin pushed out his bottom lip, frowning. "That's a possibility," he admitted. "Those raptors made quick work of our ambushers, so they are probably wondering what happened to them."

"How do you think we should get in there?" I asked. Pine needles beneath me pricked my hands. The squad of soldiers didn't appear to be the trusting type, and they were too numerous to sneak by.

"It won't be through the front door," Sargin said, pulling out his canteen, then chugging a gulp.

We snuck back to the rendezvous where the rest of the group had also returned from conducting reconnaissance of their own. After hearing our report, the group decided that a front-door approach would not work.

Hazi's findings gave us the most optimistic option. She scouted out the south side of Untermeth where the gate opened into vast fields of crop and farmlands. She led us there, where we hid in the trees, observing the farmhands working.

"It seems the past does nothing small," I said, observing the massive-sized crops being harvested.

An amalgam of races worked the fields together in harmony, including giants. Some people were picking crops while others burned brush in pits. Animals chased each other in play up and down the cultivated fields. A giant watched a dog pass by as he picked a grape from a vine and popped it in his mouth.

Beyond the farms, a group of people carrying spears and wearing animal skins wandered about. I got a closer look with my scope. They were shorter than many of the people working in the field, but they appeared to have stout bodies. *Were these the prehistoric people I learned about in school?*

"Are you looking for work?" asked a man from behind us.

We spun around to see a dwarf holding a shovel with both hands.

"Work?" Malah asked.

"Yes," the dwarf answered. "Do you need work?" The dwarf showed no suspicion about our mysterious behavior or my odd clothing.

"We were just trying to find shelter for the night," Sargin said, thinking quickly.

The dwarf stepped forward, angling the shovel handle toward a field. "Well, I'm behind picking from my garden, thanks to all those quakes lately, so I could use some assistance," he said. "Help me out, and I can give you shelter for the evening."

"We're a bit tired," Hazi said, wiping the leaves and pine needles off her clothes, "but I think I have it in me to give you a hand."

The dwarf scratched the hair above his forehead. "When you speak," he said to Hazi, "your mouth moves with your words." He pointed the shovel to the rest of the party. "With everyone else, I don't hear your words right away."

Sargin stood up and approached the dwarf, holding out his hand with a friendly gesture. "We'd love to tell you the story."

The short man grinned, then took Sargin's hand and shook firmly. "I, in turn, would love that. I'm Abydemus," he said as though he was thirsty for new tales around a campfire. Abydemus looked at Andros. "You may not get along too well here, my friend, with a head like that," the dwarf said, tapping his forehead. "I have something you can wear."

"You realize that this guy is a reptilian," Hazi said, putting a hand on Andros's shoulder.

"Okay," Abydemus said, lifting his shoulders. "You trust him, so I trust him."

"Are you serious?" Sargin asked him.

Abydemus ignored the comment and waved his hand for us to follow.

With any possible wall of distrust crumbled, Abydemus took us to his fields. Like a good host, Abydemus offered Andros a cloak, which was accepted with gratitude. Baugi was a pleasant surprise for Abydemus. He cleared logs and took on many tasks that could not be accomplished by the dwarf's hindered size.

"Finally able to hire some help, I see," a nearby farmer said to Abydemus, thumbs tucked into his pockets. Abydemus waved at the man with a smile and both men returned to their work.

We picked fruits, dug up vegetables, and loaded the produce onto several carts. Once loaded, Abydemus tied the carts together, and Baugi pulled them through the city gates. We followed close behind.

Abydemus brought us to a stand where Baugi parked the carts. We helped Abydemus display his crops for customers to inspect and buy. For several hours, Abydemus took customers' money with giddy excitement. With each purchase, we helped the patrons load up their carts while others in our party replenished the produce on the table for display.

A tall blond-haired man entered the booth, rubbing his jaw. "I see you are doing well today, nephew," he said.

Abydemus ran to the man, who quickly knelt and gave an affectionate familial embrace. "Best day yet, thanks to my help," he said, holding his hand out toward us.

"Thank you for helping my nephew," the blond man said standing up. "He may be short, but I've never seen a person work as hard as he does."

Abydemus rolled his eyes, giggling and enjoying his small fortune.

"He worked me under the table," I said, wanting to fuel the positive emotions.

The uncle snapped his head back. "Interesting," he said, likely referring to the delay in translation. "Why would Abydemus work you there?" he asked.

"What?" I asked, not understanding the question.

"Stupid translator," the doctor said. Then I heard a thud in the background.

I continued. "I said he worked me under the table, as in, I worked hard."

"Oh," the uncle said, "I understand."

"They are staying with me tonight, Uncle," Abydemus blurted. "Do you want to join us for dinner? It will be a great feast!"

"Count me in," the uncle said, then dropped a hand on the dwarf's shoulder and returned his attention to me and the rest of my party. "Among many things, I'm a doctor in this town. When I come by, I should be able to take care of some of those wounds," he said, pointing to the various black marks, scratches, cuts, and more. "The name is Gaylin."

Gaylin glanced at Andros and produced a lopsided grin but said nothing about him. He said his goodbyes, then left.

"Do you think he is going to turn us in to the authorities?" Malah asked, not worried about the presence of the patrons.

"What authorities?" Abydemus asked, taking money from a customer.

"The patrols in the forest," Sargin clarified, pointing in the direction of the front gate. "We ran into a few of them."

"Oh, those are just adventurers," he said nonchalantly. "If you enter the wrong part of the forest, you are free game to them. If you killed them, that is their own doing."

"What part of the forest is the wrong part?" Hazi asked the dwarf.

"Out past the river," Abydemus said, waving a hand outward.

"With the raptors?" I asked, wondering why anybody with sanity would risk their lives in such a foolish manner.

Abydemus gave me a quizzical look. "What raptors?" he asked with sarcasm. I sensed he knew exactly what I was talking about.

Abydemus dropped his elbows on a table and folded his arms. "Our people and her people used to be one and the same," he said, nodding toward Hazi. "She's among the warrior elite."

"What's your point?" Hazi asked, surprised by Abydemus's observation.

"Adventurers sometimes rescue people in the forest from certain death. They've found several who were injured during their trials," he said, nodding at Hazi.

"Is that how you keep tabs on us?" Hazi asked.

"We don't really care what you do, and that isn't the point," Abydemus answered. "All I'm saying is that our adventurers like being heroes, but they are such an unpredictable bunch. And they always have great stories to tell. I'm not sure if they are true, but they make for great entertainment."

"I'll bet," Hazi commented while lifting a basket.

"We've done well here," the dwarf said. "Heck! We've made peace with giants, whereas you, on the other hand, still hunt them," he accused. Abydemus glanced at Baugi. "Then again, it seems like you made peace with a giant too." The small man gave Hazi an approving nod.

"You're happy here," Sargin said with admiration.

Abydemus took the comment as a compliment. "Don't get me wrong," he laughed. "We have our problems."

We continued to assist our host, and when the day waned, we closed the market booth, and Abydemus took his earnings and purchased wine and meat. Then he led us to his humble abode. Baugi stooped to enter the front door. Abydemus took the cloak from Andros and offered the reptilian a seat. We lit fires in two stoves and helped Abydemus prepare a feast.

"You seem to be enjoying yourself," Andros said to Abydemus.

"Oh, I am," he assured. "Thanks to all of you, I've had the best day at the shop this season. To top it off, I have guests to help me enjoy my small fortune!"

Abydemus poured us drinks, and we partook. His pure joy penetrated our spirits, and we forgot all the troubles of the world. Abydemus proved to be a kind soul who took pleasure in entertaining guests and filling their bellies with good food and drink.

I did not want the evening to end, but as with all things, reality rears its ugly head.

Our reality came knocking on the door.

CHAPTER 30

Abydemus opened the door, where Gaylin stood holding a plate covered with a piece of cloth. Gaylin removed the cloth and revealed a block of cheese with a chunk cut out. Several smaller morsels were piled on the plate, ready to serve.

"I brought your favorite," Gaylin teased.

Abydemus snatched a morsel and bit into it. His face softened into ecstasy as he chewed. He then took a swig of wine. "Do you remember my uncle?" he asked us.

We greeted him. Gaylin wasted no time taking the wine bottle from Abydemus and pouring himself a glass. He sipped some, then noticed the reptilian in the room. Andros, who had been drinking a considerable amount, gave Gaylin a small wave. Gaylin returned the greeting with a curt wave of his own. He finished his wine in one gulp and placed his empty glass on the table beside me, looking me over.

Gaylin held out his hands toward my head. "May I?" he asked, indicating he wanted to check for something.

"Sure," I said.

Gaylin examined my head and stopped when he found the bump in the back of it. "Something was inserted in there," he said, pouring another glass of wine.

"What's on your mind?" I asked.

Gaylin let out a short laugh. "Your mind, in fact," he said. "You see, I've done some research on the brain and its telepathic abilities. I gave up, but after meeting you, I'm getting a little curious again." Gaylin sipped from his cup. "Where are you from?"

"Wrong question. More like when," I answered, acting on the buzz from the wine. "I've traveled back in time, but how far, I can't even guess."

"Have you always had that bump on the back of your head?" he asked.

"No," I answered. "I noticed it after arriving from the future."

"Do you remember your journey through time?" he inquired.

"No."

Gaylin snapped his fingers. "The incision in your head. Someone surgically placed something in your skull. A transmitter, I assume."

Everyone in the room listened with interest, including Baugi, who sat sprawled out on the floor, chugging goblets of wine.

I rubbed the bump. "So they did put something in me," I muttered.

He nodded. "Who's listening to you, I wonder?"

"I talk to someone who calls himself 'doctor,'" I confirmed.

"Interesting," Gaylin said, hunching over. "To many, this is known as the Second Age. Does that mean anything to you?"

"In a way," I answered. "The doctor, the guy who talks to me from the future, also mentioned that this was the Second Age."

"So that guy from the future can hear you now?" Gaylin asked, fidgeting in his seat, seeking confirmation.

"I assume so," I answered, but not quite sure.

Gaylin slouched. "How far back do you think you've traveled?"

"I don't know." I stood up and paced the floor, shoving my hands into my pockets. "And apparently, neither does the doctor."

"Then how did you get here?" he asked.

This question elicited a response from the doctor, who had been listening to the conversation and gave me an explanation.

"The Second Age, or this age," I corrected myself, relaying the doctor's explanation, "is kind of lost in time. He got me here using fixed points, whatever that means." I held up my hands, surrendering to my lack of understanding. "He described it as using a magnet to find a needle in a haystack."

"I wonder if you're connected to that object orbiting our planet." Gaylin contemplated.

Sargin stood and joined me in pacing, then snapped his fingers. "The scroll," he blurted. "Maybe the scroll had something to do with it."

"The doctor said it's time locked," I said.

"That's how they got you here," Sargin said. "The time lock probably served as a beacon of sorts."

"If that is so, then why don't they know precisely where it is, and more importantly, why not just drop me off by it?" I asked.

"Good question," Sargin said. "Though time and space may be interconnected, they aren't the same, and the universe is in constant motion. The location of our planet now is not the same place as it will be in the future. Simply put, you didn't travel just through time, but through space also. It is an incredible feat."

"You are hurting my head," I said, trying to keep up with his rationale. He did have a point. The stars at night, though similar, did appear different than in my time. It was like they were closer, more crowded. *How far back did I travel to notice such a difference? Perhaps there isn't much difference, and I am just imagining things.*

Hazi sat directly in front of me, raising one eyebrow. She opened her mouth to speak but decided to eat a cheese cube instead and pass the plate around. Baugi picked up the block, attempting to eat it whole, but Hazi pulled it away from him, sliced off some of the cheese, and gave that piece to him.

The dishes in the kitchen began rattling and clanging just as a painting fell off the wall. Everyone dove for cover as a quake rolled through. Abydemus hit his head on the corner of the table, then fell backward into the wall. Blood streamed down his face. A wood brace cracked in the ceiling so loud I thought we had been hit by a lightning strike. Hazi, seeing the danger above, scrambled to Abydemus and dragged him out of the way. The timber cracked again, then fell to the floor where Abydemus had been a few moments before.

The rumblings and quaking eased. All around, dust filled the air, causing several of us to choke and cough. Sargin made his rounds with each person, making sure his party was uninjured. Gaylin tended to Abydemus's head wound. He stopped the bleeding with a rag, then pulled out a packet from his belt, opened it, and rubbed a powder on the wound.

"I forgot. You're a doctor." I half joked, wiping the dust off me.

"These quakes are only going to get worse," Gaylin warned.

"Worse than that," Andros said. "We're running out of time."

"You've got a point," Sargin said, helping Malah to his feet, then knelt beside Gaylin. "We need to get to Midlatica," he said to Gaylin. "Can you help us?" Sargin rubbed his forearm.

"Why Midlatica?" Gaylin asked, putting a bandage on Abydemus's head.

"The scroll Sargin told you about," I said, "it's there."

Gaylin helped his nephew to his feet, instructing him to keep pressure on the head wound. "The scroll." He echoed. "Not exactly a scroll though, is it?"

"What do you mean?" I asked.

"There are four scrolls you are looking for," Gaylin said. "At one point, they were lost in time and space. Three still are, but the Midlaticans found the first scroll during the First Age. Even if you find it, what would it matter?"

"A fool's errand, then?" Malah asked, letting out a sigh.

"My father did not send us on a fool's errand," Sargin defended.

Gaylin urged his nephew to rest a little more, then stood up to face Sargin. "Not a fool's errand," he said. "It's worth an attempt. With the reptilians gone, we might have a chance to reach it now." Gaylin then glanced at Andros. "Well, most reptilians."

Andros found no humor in the joke. "The reptilians may have left, but whoever destroyed Ganteep One is still out there."

"One problem at a time," Gaylin said, taking a seat on the dusty couch. "I can get us transportation."

"What if we get there and find that the scroll is under lock and key?" I asked.

"Like I said, one problem at a time. We'll worry about that when we get there," Gaylin said. "First thing we need to do is make our way to Midlatica."

"We?" Malah highlighted the choice of Gaylin's words.

"I'm going with you," Gaylin said, standing. "We've got something that should work. Heck, it will even hold your dragon." Gaylin grinned. "According to our sky observers, he's heading south, so we can pick him up en route."

"How do you know so much?" Sargin asked.

"He's also the mayor," Abydemus said, touching his wound with his fingers, then inspecting them to make sure there was no blood.

"You're the town doctor and the mayor?" I asked.

"I wanted a new challenge," Gaylin said. "After treating people for a couple of centuries, I *needed* a new challenge."

"I forgot. You guys live a long time," I uttered with disappointment in my own short life span.

Malah was less amused with Gaylin's willingness to leave. "Sounds like you are abandoning your people." Malah accused.

"And you didn't?" Gaylin retorted. "Listen, there is nothing I can do for my people here anymore. Maybe with you, I can do some good."

"Great!" Sargin said. "Take us to our transport."

"Oh no," Gaylin corrected. "It's not that easy. It's under military control. We may have to steal it! Don't worry. I have a friend who might be able to help."

"We eat first," Baugi said, licking his lips at the feast littering the wrecked floor.

I looked at the mess and patted the giant on the back. "I don't think the ten-second rule applies here, my friend."

CHAPTER 31
NIGHT

The roads were dim, lit by only the occasional streetlight that had survived the quakes. City workers hoisted themselves atop poles to inspect the damage with helmet lights and equipment. Debris littered the paths, but the mood of the town felt lighthearted. The pubs were filled with laughter.

Gaylin led us through a series of streets, then down an alley. I heard music playing a somber tune ahead. The music grew louder the more we walked, until we came upon another street, and the music ceased abruptly. Pub doors flapped open, and a drunken man stumbled out, gripping a bottle. The drunkard tripped, fell to the ground, and passed out. The bottle spilled its contents, wetting the man's face. The music resumed. The citizens of Untermeth were either naive to their apocalyptic fate, or they didn't care.

The street occupants gave us evening greetings, and we continued unhindered. We diverted down another alley where a beggar held out a metal cup. Gaylin dropped a few coins in it, then pressed on.

"Who goes there?" an invisible figure asked.

"An old friend," Gaylin answered, straightening his back.

"You made it," the man said, stepping into the light.

The men shook hands, and then Gaylin made introductions. "Everybody, this is Eudoxus."

We stood frozen, piecing the puzzle together. It was now clear that Gaylin had a plan.

"Obviously, I got your message, but what's going on?" Eudoxus asked.

"The attacks on Ganteep City were confirmed, and I'm assuming that half a billion citizens were killed," Gaylin said.

"Half a billion?" I blurted with shock. "In one city?"

"It was a big city," Malah said.

"That's bigger than my country," I murmured to myself.

Eudoxus watched the interchange between Malah and me, with apparent recognition that our communication was facilitated by some form of technology, but said nothing.

"We need to get these people out of here," Gaylin said. "Everything that's been happening. The attack. The quakes. It's all interconnected."

"What are you saying?" Eudoxus asked, unable to hide the suspicion on his face. "These guys are the cause?"

Gaylin shook his head. "I believe they hold our only hope."

"Hope?" Eudoxus asked, inspecting our motley crew. "Hope for what?"

"Any glimmer of a future for man," Sargin said, interjecting without pomp. "This world is coming to an end."

"You know that, do you?" he asked, pulling on his cuffs. "Perhaps we can organize an offensive."

"With whom? Our only chance was Ganteep, and they got their asses handed to them," Gaylin said, shooting down the idea.

"I know," he answered. Eudoxus recognized Sargin. "I knew your father. In fact, I once called him a friend before our falling out. It's easy to recognize someone who looks so human when their father is not. I'm assuming he's dead."

"Possibly. I didn't see my father die," Sargin said. I wasn't sure if he was holding out hope or just staying focused on the mission. However, he had a point. We didn't physically see King Sar die.

Eudoxus, who towered over us all except Baugi, lifted a finger for all to be silent. He turned his attention to me and scowled. My knees bent, feeling wobbly with the sudden attention of the stranger. I blinked back, trying to maintain eye contact. "You are putting a lot of faith in him." Eudoxus held out his hand toward me.

"Feeling suspicious?" Gaylin joked.

Eudoxus shook his head. "What's your plan?"

"Steal something that will fly us out of here," Gaylin burst out.

Surprise filled his whole face. "One of my planes?" Eudoxus affirmed.

"Not a plane," Gaylin said with a sheepish grin.

"You are out of your damn mind." Eudoxus threw up his arms in disbelief. "You do realize that you have a reptilian and a giant with you, don't you?" he asked, pointing out the obvious as though he just revealed something new of significance.

"Don't forget the dragon," Abydemus added, still putting pressure on his head with a piece of cloth.

Eudoxus fixed his eyes on Sargin. "And a king," he said in contemplation. He cleared his throat. "Okay then. Why not. It's fit for a king," he said shaking his head. "Hell, it's fit for a dragon too."

***

The clouds blanketed the stars above and projected a glow from the city lights of Untermeth below. We approached a high fence topped off with barbed wire. Sentries stood in guard towers spaced out along the perimeter.

The guards at the gates recognized Eudoxus and let him and the rest of us through without resistance, albeit with surprise at seeing both a giant and a reptilian up close. We crossed a cement courtyard to a tunnel entrance that burrowed through a cliff. Baugi stepped inside without having to hunch over. The tunnel floor slanted downward deep below the surface. Corridors branched off from the main tunnel, but we kept our path straight. We reached a vast opening, pillared with stalagmites and stalactites. Within the spacious cavity, more soldiers guarded a cement wall with a single door.

One of the soldiers spoke with Eudoxus, then led us to the barrier where he swiped a card over a control panel. The door opened, and he let us through, locking us in. We stepped into an underground flight line and came face-to-face with a ship whose image had burnt itself into my brain for all eternity. It was a rectangular black ship with the same configuration as those we witnessed destroy Outpost One. This craft, though large, appeared smaller than the ones we saw earlier. It hovered in front of us with a ladder attached.

"Did you—" I started, but Eudoxus, who anticipated my question, cut me off.

"No," Eudoxus assured.

"What?" asked Malah, eyeing Eudoxus with the same suspicions I had.

"He was going to ask if we destroyed the Ganteep outpost. We didn't," Eudoxus affirmed.

"How do you know about that?" Malah asked.

"Because I'm competent," Eudoxus answered.

"Did you build that ship?" I asked.

"No," Gaylin answered for Eudoxus. "We recovered it during an archeological excavation. We believe it crashed."

"And this is your idea of a transport?" Malah scoffed.

"Would you like me to find you a luxury liner?" Eudoxus shot back. "This thing is far more advanced than anything else we have, and it is large enough for your dragon if we can find him."

I felt a small rumble. "Is there heavy machinery below us?" I asked out loud.

The lights flickered, and dirt fell from the ceiling. My muscles quivered with anticipation. I didn't have to wait long. The ground rocked, knocking me off balance. I lunged toward the ladder, holding on to it with all my strength. A stalactite from the ceiling broke free.

"Let's move!" Eudoxus yelled.

The ladder rattled violently, throwing me to the floor. Baugi, who braced himself by grabbing a ledge of the ship, tossed me inside along with my companions. Baugi was smacked in the head by the hull, causing blood to gush over his eye bandage. Another tremor knocked his feet out from under him. He reached for a rung on the ladder, but the ceiling cracked, causing a boulder to fall and roll onto his leg. The giant cried out in pain.

Hazi and Andros jumped out of the ship and scrambled on all fours to reach Baugi. Lying on their backs and using their legs to push the boulder, they freed the giant. His leg was broken.

Baugi used his arms and pulled himself to the ladder amidst the rolling quakes. Hazi and Andros pushed the giant upward while we pulled on him. With incredible strength, the giant lifted himself into the craft, with his leg flopping halfway down the thigh. Hazi and Andros scrambled up the ladder, then shut the door.

"Go now!" Gaylin yelled to the cockpit, and the ship accelerated down a corridor of the cave, out a vast opening, and into the air. Behind us, the wall turned into a screen. The ground opened beneath Untermeth and sucked the city into a newly formed abyss.

"Is this how it all ends?" I asked, not convinced salvation was possible. "I want to go home."

Hazi squeezed my shoulder. "Me too," she said, then turned her attention back to Baugi, who was now passed out on the floor of the ship.

Gaylin forced the giant's bone back into place, setting it. With two metal rods, he splinted the leg.

Abydemus, with teary eyes, stared out the window. Sargin, sensitive to what Abydemus must be feeling, knelt beside the dwarf and put a friendly hand on his shoulder.

"We're clear," Eudoxus yelled from the cockpit.

"Set course for Midlatica," Gaylin answered. He turned to me. "Are you ready to see the center of the planet?"

PART IV

CHAPTER 32
LATE NIGHT

Nothing. I felt absolutely nothing.

The vessel flew as if in a bubble, freeing us from experiencing any acceleration or turbulence.

Unlike the matte appearance outside, the inside was sleek, with no sharp edges except for several mechanical and electronic attachments installed by Untermeth scientists and engineers. Wires and cords stretched uniformly along the floor leading into the cockpit. Toward the rear, the cabin grew spacious. If we found Enkidu, he'd travel comfortably lying on the floor of the ship.

The passenger cabin was connected to the cockpit, separated by a wall with an open entrance. Chairs protruded from the floor as if the entire room had been produced from a single mold. Abydemus sat comfortably in one of the seats, dangling his feet.

I took a seat next to the dwarf and let my thoughts run freely in my mind. At first, I pondered on the similarities between this ship and the ones that destroyed Ganteep Outpost One. Then the memory of my father, pictured on the screen at the outpost, left me in contemplation. *How could my father be here? Is this a dream?*

The doctor's voiced chimed in. "This isn't a dream, Keiji."

None of this makes any sense. There's no logic to it, I responded, watching Abydemus nod off. *Or maybe I just don't know what is logical anymore.*

"Good," the doctor said. "You're learning."

The doctor's response irritated me, so I decided to change the venue and headed to the cockpit where Eudoxus sat, flying the ship. "Have a seat," he offered, without looking back at me.

I sat to his right, inspecting the jumble of makeshift panels before me, complete with dashboards, electronic displays, and a mixture of buttons and toggle switches. Unlike the rest of the ship, the cockpit was completely revamped with modern technology. The only things not altered were the transparent walls, roof, and floor, giving the crew an unobstructed view all around with overlaying electronic trajectories displayed. "Who built this ship?" I asked fiddling with my lighter.

"We don't know," Eudoxus answered, not offering to speculate.

Bending my elbows, I slouched. "Do you have any suspicions?"

"Some of our scientists believe this ship is from the First Age," Eudoxus said, typing on a panel within the dash.

"Any bodies inside when y'all found it?" I asked, rubbing my ear.

"What's *y'all*?" he asked. "Is your translator broken?"

"Sorry. *You*," I corrected. "Were there any bodies inside when *you* found the ship?"

"No," he said, leaning over to check the ground below him. "None that I know of, but we discovered a recording in the memory banks of this ship that was still intact."

Eudoxus typed some symbols into a keyboard. A holographic figure of a brown-haired, green-eyed man appeared in the cabin before us. He was wearing a dark-blue jacket with brass buttons lining the front. Each sleeve was embroidered with six thin stripes. His outfit was reminiscent of a navy officer from the nineteenth century. He spoke. "Single entry. We found and hid the object. Mission was a success. Captain Elton Blake of the *Gideon* signing off." The holograph vanished.

Eudoxus rubbed his hands on the side of his face, hunching over to rest his elbows on the console. "I've heard this message many times, but I never had a clue what he was saying." He covered his mouth, eyeing me. "That translator in your head is quite something."

I was also astonished, but for a different reason. "That was English," I said, noting no time delay in what was being said. "In fact, that was very much an American English dialect."

Eudoxus shifted in his seat. "Then we have another piece of the puzzle," he said, pondering. "I'm not sure what it means, but at least we now have a name for this ship." Eudoxus patted the console. "The *Gideon*."

The man in the holographic image was speaking English. Who is Captain Elton Blake? Was he the same Blake whom Sar gave me the message for? Why was he on an alien ship that crashed during the First Age? What was his mission?

I waited for a response from the doctor, but I was left sitting in silence. "You believe this ship crashed during the First Age, eh?" I asked.

"Supposedly," Eudoxus said, nonchalantly.

"If you think it is from the First Age, then I'm assuming you have an idea as to how old the ship is?" I asked, trying to stir up a conversation.

"Tens of thousands of years," Eudoxus replied. "Who knows."

I rose from my chair and laid my hand on the transparent wall. It was smooth to the touch. "But this looks and feels brand new." Raindrops outside splattered across the hull. Beyond the rain, turbulent waters of an ocean met with dark clouds. The water swelled up high. "How big are those waves?" I asked, pointing to the ocean.

He flipped a toggle switch, then punched in a button. "Gigantic," he answered. "Between the storm, earthquakes, and tsunamis, the coast will be destroyed." A light on one of his makeshift panels blinked, so he touched it. "That's interesting," he said, turning the ship a nudge to the right. "Something, or someone, is flying ahead."

Eudoxus dropped altitude and leveled off behind a gliding dragon. It was Enkidu! We flew closer, shortening the gap between the dragon and our ship.

"He's got to be exhausted," I said.

"I agree. He's losing altitude," Eudoxus said, punching in buttons and accelerating the craft. "If he can't pull up, he will be caught in one of those waves." Eudoxus swept past the dragon. "Go to the back and help him aboard. If you open the cargo bay, he should be able to glide in. Hurry!"

I raced from the cockpit to the passenger cabin, apprising our small fellowship of the situation. "We found Enkidu. We are going to try and bring him on board through the cargo bay."

"That's crazy," Abydemus said, standing up.

There was no time to argue. "More than crazy," I replied. "It's nuts, but if we don't hurry, one of the tsunamis will envelop him."

Malah jumped up. "How do we open the cargo bay?" he asked, wasting no time.

"Follow me," Gaylin motioned, already sprinting to the back.

We left Baugi behind and reached the back of the craft where the cargo bay was situated. It was filled with crates that needed to be moved out of the way if we were to bring in a dragon.

"What's with all this stuff?" I asked, frustrated at the obstacle ahead.

"It's a cargo ship," Gaylin yelled, "so don't ask stupid questions. Secure the crates to the sides," he said, directing his finger toward Andros, Hazi, and Sargin.

Without argument, they got to work.

"Abydemus," Gaylin called.

"Here!" the dwarf answered.

"Get to the control panel and, when I give the signal, open the bay doors."

"Gotcha," Abydemus said, then ran to the wall that housed the control panel.

"Malah," Gaylin called, "you guide Enkidu in."

Malah positioned himself in the center with a direct line of sight to the rear of the craft.

"Everything is secured," Sargin informed Gaylin.

Gaylin slapped an intercom button on the wall opposite of Abydemus. "We're set," Gaylin announced to Eudoxus. "Are you in position?"

"Yes," Eudoxus confirmed over the speaker. "Open the cargo bay now!"

Gaylin pointed to Abydemus, who in turn punched a button.

The cargo bay doors opened slowly. Outside, Enkidu appeared to be on the verge of floundering, with only the vertical wall of a giant wave as his backdrop.

Malah tried to direct Enkidu in, but the dragon was wavering, unable to gain enough speed. "We need to slow down!" Malah screamed.

Eudoxus complied, slowing the ship. Enkidu's wings collapsed against his torso, and he shot into the cargo bay, sliding like a wet fish to a stop before crashing into Malah. The dragon wheezed, trying to catch his breath.

Abydemus punched the button again, and the bay doors began to close slowly. The huge wave was rapidly chasing us.

"Get us out of here!" Gaylin yelled into the intercom.

We watched the wave shrink behind us through the closing doors. I sat down, letting out a sigh of relief. Everyone else did the same, except for Andros, who was still pacing. He stopped and shook his head. "I think I just pissed my pants."

CHAPTER 33
DAWN OF THE SIXTH DAY

Gaylin used the *Gideon*'s medical facilities to fuse the bones in Baugi's leg back together. Sargin replaced Eudoxus in the cockpit while the rest of us slept.

My mother took my hands. "You must remember," she said, wearing a traditional Japanese garment. "We are very fortunate."

"Why are we fortunate, Mother?" I asked, gently squeezing her hands in return.

"Why do you ask that, when you know the answer? You know where you are, don't you?" she asked.

"I'm home in Kokura," I answered. "Kokura, Japan." I shook my head. "Don't be dramatic, Mother. That happened a long time ago."

"No, Keiji," she corrected. "It hasn't happened yet, but it still can." My mother wept. "So much innocence, lost."

A bright flash burst from the sky, and an explosion threw me backward into the side of a hill. I scrambled to my feet to watch my hometown evaporate in an atomic explosion.

"That's not right," I said.

"What's not?" a man asked, placing a hand on my shoulder.

"Kokura wasn't destroyed," I answered.

The man crossed over to stand before me. His military uniform displayed his name, Hudson. I met his gray eyes, standing face-to-face with my father, Michael Hudson. "You are both right and wrong," he said, placing his other hand on my shoulder, too. "It's all connected." His uniform was replaced with that of Admiral Radau, but the face remained the same. "I'm with you, Keiji," he said, squeezing my shoulder. "I'm always with you."

I woke up and rolled over to a tray full of nuts and fruits. Malah had opened some crates and found food. After eating, I ventured into the cockpit, where Sargin was flying the ship. Eudoxus was on the floor trying to sleep. Through the clear floor, dark clouds blocked the light of dawn, but the luminescent crashing of salt water was visible below.

A light on the dash blinked. "We are arriving at the entrance," Sargin said, then nudged Eudoxus with his foot.

Eudoxus awoke and waddled his way into the copilot's seat, rubbing his eyes. He tapped a display, then punched a button. "It's been a long time since any of our people have been here," he said. "Any ideas on how to get in?"

In response, my bracelet warmed and began to glow. A spinning vortex opened into the ocean.

Instinctively, Sargin pointed the ship to the middle of the vortex, and we entered it. The passage felt like it was an infinite wall of spinning water. I felt dizzy, so I sat on the floor. Except for Baugi and Enkidu, our companions joined us.

The vortex morphed into a tunnel, and we traveled through a void of blackness. I was suddenly struck with a coldness, as if I stepped into a walk-in freezer. The sensation lasted only a few seconds. "What was that?" I asked.

"I'm not sure," Sargin responded.

We exited the tunnel into a cavernous, glowing realm. The sky was lit by the luminescent water swirling above, covering the inside globe of the Earth as if gravity had reversed itself.

Hanging on nothing within a hollow Earth was a smaller planet. Sargin brought us in closer. Its surface was covered by a thick forest.

Sargin leveled the ship, flying only a few feet above the treetops. Eudoxus plotted a course, and the ship flew toward a cluster of lights gleaming in the distance.

The speaker screamed an alarm that was unmistakably a warning. Two fighter jets with crescent-shaped wings buzzed us, then circled back on our tails.

"Those things are armed to the teeth," Eudoxus said.

The intercom light blinked. Sargin flipped a toggle switch. Somebody was speaking on the other end, but the language was not decipherable.

Eudoxus began toggling a switch. The newcomers blinked their lights at us, as if using some sort of Morse Code. Whatever the message was that we sent, it appeared to be accepted by our new arrivals. They flanked the *Gideon* and escorted us to the city ahead.

"What did you do?" I asked Eudoxus.

"I basically said that we don't mean any harm." He glanced at the crafts on either side. "If we veer off from this path, they will open fire."

"The old 'I come in peace' bit, eh?" I joked. "Seems like we could fly laps around those jets."

"It's best not to get cocky," Gaylin warned. "Somebody else may be watching."

"Like whom?" I asked.

"Like whoever is in those towers," Eudoxus pointed to several tall structures with spotlights. We slowed down and passed the tower closest to us. Along with the spotlight, the tower supported an installation of cannons.

"Those cannons are likely able to take us down quickly," he said, then patted the control panel. "Our scientists speculated that it is possible that the *Gideon* was shot down."

"Shot down?" I asked.

"Much of the repairs we made were consistent with a battle-damaged ship," Gaylin said.

Lights ahead grew brighter as cross streets below became visible. The jet fighters escorted us to an open area where runways extended in three different directions. We received coordinates via a diagram on a display panel, so Sargin directed the ship accordingly. We slowed, descended, and parked on a landing pad, bringing our ship to a rest.

"Keiji," the doctor whispered in my head.

"Yeah," I responded.

Everyone spun, watching me. I tapped my temple, indicating that the doctor was speaking.

"Keep the dragon on board and don't let the Midlaticans enter the ship," the doctor warned.

I gave the warning to the rest of the crew.

"I will stay with Enkidu and keep him calm," Malah volunteered.

"Baugi still needs some rest," Gaylin said, turning to Hazi. "He trusts you. Will you stay with him?"

Hazi tightened her grip on her spear, dropped her chin with acceptance of her assignment, and then returned to the sleeping giant.

"What does the doctor say about Andros?" Sargin asked, tapping a finger on the reptilian's shoulder.

"The doctor said nothing," I answered.

"I don't like it," Sargin said. "With everything that has happened, I think it would be best if he stays with the *Gideon*."

The reptilian protested with a grunt but succumbed to the logic and joined Hazi.

Eudoxus hit a button and lowered a ramp from just behind the cockpit.

"If we had this, then why that ladder at Untermeth?" I asked with sarcasm.

"We were doing maintenance," Eudoxus answered and then headed out. A squad of pale-skinned human soldiers greeted us, each carrying a sidearm and a sword. Their black uniforms were embroidered with gold filigree on the shoulders and cuffs. At the far end of the flight line, soldiers wearing red coats stood at attention with weapons in hand.

One of the guards spoke, but the language was still indecipherable. With sword in hand, he pointed us beyond the redcoats. The guard spoke again, but still my head could not translate. Suddenly, a rush of emotions emitted from him. The most predominant feeling was that of anger.

"Please," the guard urged, tightening his lips.

"I'm sorry," Sargin said, now able to interpret the guard's words. "Will you please repeat what you said?"

The guard struck the ground with his spear. His back stiffened. "Lay down your weapons and step over here, please," the guard repeated, pointing to the right.

We complied with the order. Then the guards patted us down in search of concealed weapons. The soldier nearest me pulled back my shirt sleeve, revealing the bracelet. He had an identical bracelet on his wrist. He lifted my arm for the lead guard to see, then let go, allowing my arm to fall free.

"Why do your lips not move with the words you speak? What kind of sorcery is this?" the lead guard asked.

"Because they are using a telepathic translator," came a voice from behind the guards. The guards stepped aside, allowing a bearded man to approach us. "I apologize for the harsh welcome," he said. "My name is Berossus." He held out his hand, and each of us shook it. Each time he gave our wrists a small twist, inspecting the bracelets that some of us wore, but said nothing.

"Are you aware of what has been happening on the surface?" Sargin asked.

Berossus didn't answer the question immediately. "You're the son of Sar," he stated. He stepped back, then answered Sargin's question. "We are aware of what's been happening."

"Why didn't you help us?" Sargin asked.

"Not our fight. However, that ship has the emperor quite intrigued," Berossus said, referring to the *Gideon*.

Sargin stood upright. "May we see your emperor?" he asked.

"Of course," Berossus answered.

Something unnerved me about Berossus. I felt nothing emanate from him emotionally, like someone was blocking my empathic ability. I wasn't sure what to make of our predicament, but one feeling persisted: we weren't welcomed guests.

CHAPTER 34
EARLY MORNING

The doors opened to a throne room with pillars rising into an unseen roof. Even the walls were lost in shadows. At least two dozen pillars separated us from the throne of a ruler. Berossus ushered us in. Our footsteps echoed as we walked on the smooth marble floor.

Though not cuffed, we were pushed forward with the tips of swords like we were prisoners. A tingle raced up my spine when I heard the familiar snorts and snarls of feroxraptors reverberate in the pitch-black background beyond the pillars.

Once we reached the other side of the room, we halted. A pale, slender man with short blond hair and blue eyes dressed in flowing red robes entered and took a position before the throne. He was followed by an entourage that included a young woman dressed in royal garments. She also had blond hair and blue eyes, except her hair was longer and in braids. She stood by the red-robed man.

Berossus bowed to the man in front of the throne, then turned his attention toward us. "This is Emperor Magnus of Midlatica," he announced. Berossus then waved a hand toward the young woman standing by the throne. "With him is his sister, Livia."

We bowed.

"Heads up," Magnus ordered, annoyed. "Where did you get that ship?" He was referring to the *Gideon.*

The sudden question caught us off guard, so the emperor repeated himself. His voice quivered with anger, and his face reddened and dripped with perspiration.

"We found it," Sargin answered, raising his arms, which lifted his sleeves and exposed his wrists.

Magnus tightened his lips with fury. "That is not your bracelet," he yelled, then pointed past us, "and that is not your ship!"

"I'm sorry," Sargin said, shifting his weight to his left, "but does the ship belong to you?"

"Are you questioning me, Sargin?" The emperor asked. It was clear that our visit wasn't completely unexpected. "Do you think you are a king?" The emperor leaned toward Sargin. "You are nothing. No people. No land. No army. Just nothing." Magnus exhaled, then pointed to me. "You're the translating time traveler." The emperor wiped his brow with a silk cloth, then crossed his arms.

"The emperor knows way too much," Gaylin whispered to me.

Magnus ignored Gaylin's comment with a wave and took a step toward me. "The name is Keiji, isn't it?"

I was stunned. "Yes, your excellency," I answered.

"Emperor Magnus," Sargin interjected. "What is your concern?"

Magnus tightened his face, flexing the muscles in his jaw. "You brought the Council of Nine to my doorsteps," the emperor blurted. "Oh yes. We know about that unauthorized detonation of your nuclear weapon," he said, twisting around toward his throne.

"Admiral Radau's ship was under heavy attack by an overwhelming reptilian fleet," Sargin defended. "Surely the Council of Nine understands."

"Oh, so you think the detonation was nothing more than a last-ditch effort?" the emperor asked with sarcasm.

"That was my belief," Sargin answered without raising his voice.

The emperor rolled his eyes until they fixed on Eudoxus. "How nice," he said. "An Untermeth general."

Two feroxraptors stepped out of the darkness, swaying side to side.

"Yes," Eudoxus answered, rubbing his palms against his pants nervously while eyeing the raptors.

"Tell me, General, if you are given an order that originates with the Council of Nine, do you ever disobey that order?" the emperor asked.

"It would have to be a very good reason," he answered.

"Brother," Livia said. "These are our guests. Perhaps we should treat them as such."

"Of course," Magnus said, smiling. He then pulled out a handgun from under his robes, pressed it against Eudoxus's head, and pulled the trigger. Eudoxus collapsed to the ground, dead. Livia and her entourage turned away, holding their hands to their mouths, appalled.

The emperor's sister recovered from her gasp and straightened her posture, face tight with determination, but tears streamed down her face. She glared at her brother, who in turn stared back at her with a raised eyebrow. "Perhaps you should learn your place, little sister," he said.

Whatever the emperor's state of mind was, one thing was now certain: he was a cold-blooded killer.

"You came for the scroll," Magnus said to me with a charismatic smile, putting his pistol back into its holster. "It's okay. You can tell me."

Still trembling, I nodded.

The emperor snapped his fingers and turned away. The raptors rushed to the body and began devouring Eudoxus. I held my breath, feeling helpless. Beside me, Abydemus shook in horror.

"The scroll does not and will not belong to you," Magnus said to me, pressing his hands together, then sitting on his throne. Saliva streamed down the emperor's chin, and sweat dripped from his face.

The putrid odor from the feasting raptors reached my nose just as Magnus clapped his hands with pleasure over them. "They're magnificent, aren't they?" he said, pointing at the dinosaurs. "Was he a friend of yours?" he asked Gaylin.

"I knew him," Gaylin nodded, unable to divert his attention from the carcass that was once his friend.

"It must be upsetting for you to see him die like this, isn't it?" he asked. "How about I show some compassion," Magnus offered, then pulled out his gun again and shot each raptor in the head with precision.

Magnus giggled like a child at the sight of the dead bodies. He holstered his pistol and returned his attention to Sargin. "You know what?" he asked. "I believe this general on the floor was honorable, just like your Admiral Radau. There was no way he'd detonate that weapon unless he was ordered to. He was trying to rip the fabric of space and time." His knowledge of events continued to prove disturbing.

"What's your point?" Sargin asked, not divulging any additional information.

"He wanted to send a message," Magnus answered. "I have a secret for you, young King. Radau was successful. He sent one," he whispered.

I stared at the emperor in confusion. "A message?" I asked.

"He sure did, and we intercepted it. Of course, we can't decipher it," Magnus admitted, "but it does have one word attached to it that doesn't require deciphering." The emperor grabbed my shoulder and tightened his grip. "That word was *Keiji*."

CHAPTER 35
MORNING

With flushed cheeks, Magnus waved a dismissing finger at Livia. Livia obeyed his instruction, and within seconds, the doors closed behind her, leaving only the emperor and his personal entourage.

"Why, oh why are you so important?" Magnus asked me rhetorically, pacing the floor. "You seem clueless," he said with an intent to belittle me. "What do you do for work?"

"I work at a hospital, cleaning rooms for patients," I said, dropping my head but maintaining eye contact with Magnus.

The emperor's face beamed. "You do the work of a slave, and that would make you a nobody," he snickered, then his face cringed. "You must be lying to me."

Unlike others in my travels to the past who sensed my sincerity, Magnus didn't.

"I assure you that I am not lying," I said.

"Not a slave?" Magnus said, eyeing Berossus and his black-coated guards. "A janitor then?" he joked.

"I'm not a janitor," I defended. "I help people, and it is a good way to pay the bills while I finish school."

"Are you going to be a doctor?" Magnus asked, glancing back toward Berossus, who only shrugged in response.

"No," I answered, "but I would like to help people who are sick."

The emperor faced the members of his staff. "He's from the future, and he wants to help heal people without healing people," he mocked. The group erupted with laughter. The emperor, though, did not laugh. If anything, he appeared to grow angry. Magnus strode forward rapidly and patted my cheek. "Why are you lying to me, kid?"

"Keiji's telling the truth," Sargin interjected on my behalf. "He is not here of his own will."

Magnus slapped Sargin across his mouth with surprising strength, sending Sargin to the ground.

"This is not your planet, son of Ganteep," Magnus spat. "You were never welcomed, even when you were refugees." The emperor knelt beside Sargin. "I didn't cause your timeline to explode. I'm not heartbroken about your recent tragedy either. Sar treated this system like it was his to plunder."

"That was before my time," Sargin said, still holding his face.

"Whatever. With Sar's death, we righted the wrong of having your stench on our planet," the emperor said, then spat on Sargin. "The people of Zuren are no more. All that is left is a bunch of half-breeds like yourself."

"We?" I asked.

"We, what?" the emperor asked back.

"You said *we* righted the wrong," I repeated, feeling bold. "Did you have something to do with this attack?"

"Don't be clever, kid," Magnus warned, then took a seat on his throne and arched forward, exposing his teeth with a broad grin. "The greed of Ganteep was like a disease. Even the Council of Nine supported our alliance with the reptilians. If they weren't put in check, they'd soon be invading Midlatica," Magnus said, striking the arms of his throne with his fists like a hammer. "That is something I'd never let happen."

"Conspiring with reptilians?" Gaylin hissed, breaking his silence.

"Oh, so judgmental," Magnus seethed, rolling his eyes.

Gaylin clenched his teeth together. "You brought this disaster upon us!" he yelled.

Magnus shook his head, saliva dripping from his mouth. "You brought this on yourselves!" he yelled.

Abydemus reached out to Gaylin. "Uncle, please!" he begged. "Don't get him madder than he already is."

Gaylin waved off Abydemus. The dwarf beckoned me to help silence his uncle, but there was nothing I could do.

"Maybe you should listen to the little guy," the emperor advised.

"You already killed my friend and my people," Gaylin exhorted. "What else is there to lose?"

Magnus waved two guards toward Abydemus, and they dragged the dwarf to a pillar. The taller guard knelt beside Abydemus, then sucker-punched him in the gut. The dwarf hunched over in pain, holding his stomach. Unsympathetically, the other guard grabbed the dwarf's hair and lifted him back up so the taller guard could punch again. The dwarf yelped and moaned.

"Stop it!" Gaylin begged.

But Magnus ordered his guards to keep punching.

"Stop it!"

Magnus ran forward and grabbed Gaylin by his hair and forced the dwarf's uncle to the ground. Gaylin tried to fight back, but he couldn't break free. One of the guards grabbed Gaylin's hair, allowing Magnus to let go. The emperor pulled out his pistol and pressed the barrel against Gaylin's temple. "First, the dwarf will watch you die. Then he will share your fate," Magnus said.

Gaylin spat on the emperor's face, who in turn lowered his gun and wiped his face dry with his sleeve. "Is this your idea of drama?" he asked, then pressed the barrel back against Gaylin's temple.

Abydemus screamed as Magnus pulled the trigger, but something altogether unexpected happened.

Gaylin's body rippled and was thrust backward about a dozen yards. The bullet that exited the emperor's barrel struck a black-clad guard in the chest, killing him.

"What the—" Magnus said, then repointed his gun at Gaylin and fired repeatedly. None of the bullets touched Gaylin. "That's impossible!" he screamed.

CHAPTER 36
LATER IN THE MORNING

The emperor's entourage stepped to the side, allowing a dark-robed figure to step forward. His eyes were black, his skin was white like powder, and his wide neck hinted at a muscular body beneath his clothing. He pulled back his hood to reveal thinning gray hair parted by a scar at the top of his scalp.

"What just happened, Cato?" the emperor asked the hulking, mysterious figure, showing reverence by slouching into a small bow.

"It appears we just witnessed a time loop, your excellency," Cato said, lifting an eyebrow, "which means somebody has locked this timeline."

"What?" Magnus cried, trotting to Cato. "But our portal?" he pleaded.

"Shhh," Cato said, putting his finger to his lips.

"Don't shush me," Magnus ordered, straightening his posture, then removed his robe, revealing a black military combat uniform underneath. "Will the portal still work?" Magnus asked, handing his robe to a servant.

Gaylin, hunched over in pain, stumbled to rejoin us. None of the black-uniformed guards objected. Gaylin pressed his palm to his head, trying to ease the headache he obtained from the recent attempt on his life, and managed to shift his attention to his nephew, who was now tied to the pillar with blood running down his face.

Cato waved his hand downward, trying to ease the emperor's temperament. "The portal sends people forward in time, so it doesn't matter if the timeline is locked. Perhaps we can take him to some point in the future where we can take care of business," he suggested, pointing at Gaylin.

Magnus slapped his hands together, pleased with the advice. "I want restraints on him," he ordered, and guards cuffed Gaylin's elbows together.

Cato watched Gaylin's predicament with unmoving black eyes, showing no expression. After the guards were finished with their task, Cato raised his index finger. "Perhaps we should shoot the rest. That way we'd know if any of them are protected by a time loop."

My stomach churned while watching the emperor take the advice with a grin. Magnus turned to the captain of his guards. "Execute the rest," he ordered.

Black-coated soldiers dragged us to the pillars by our hair and tied us to them with ropes pulled from nearby tapestries. Once we were securely restrained, they pointed their weapons at us.

I tried to reach out with my mind to the firing squad in a frantic attempt to sway their thinking, but my efforts were fruitless. The empathic field was limited. I could only sense the guards' loyalty to the emperor and the bloodthirsty hatred they had toward us. These blackcoats, our execution squad, weren't apathetic about our deaths; they wanted us to suffer.

The captain of the guard raised his sword, and the firing squad pointed their weapons at us.

I squeezed my eyes, waiting for the inevitable barrage of bullets. "Ready, aim ...," but the final command was never given.

I opened my eyes to see an arrow protruding through the captain's skull. The firing squad glanced at their captain, then turned to the direction whence the arrow was launched. Another arrow struck down one of the executioners while the others quickly returned fire. They only got off a few shots before they were crushed by a large stone. Baugi then stepped into the light with his spear and roared.

The remaining guards regrouped to attack the giant, but Hazi catapulted herself off the giant's back and sprayed arrow after arrow at them in midair.

Cato twirled his arm, ordering the entourage to leave the throne room. Three of the black guards grabbed Gaylin by the tunic and followed the entourage and the emperor out.

My arms were suddenly freed from the bindings. I turned around to see Andros crouched with a blade in hand. He handed me a pistol, then hurried to Sargin and Abydemus to free them also, arming them too.

Members of the emperor's army rushed into the throne room. Unlike the guards, who wore black, the emperor's army wore red coats. Hazi and Baugi wasted no time in attacking the newcomers, hurling projectiles and arrows at them. The rest of us used pillars for cover, firing on our attackers.

Baugi, undeterred by the barrage of bullets, lunged across the throne room and attacked the emperor's soldiers, crushing them with his fists and impaling them with his spear.

One of the redcoats fired a pistol at Hazi but missed. He tried again, but the weapon jammed, so he threw it to the ground and pulled out his sword, swinging at her. She parried the sword attack with her ax, then with a sudden swoop, swung her ax upward and lodged it into the man's chin, splitting his jaw in half. Hazi wasted no time recovering her ax.

The redcoats struck at Baugi, and despite his overwhelming strength, the numbers were not in his favor. His body took in bullet after bullet along with sword strike after sword strike. More soldiers raced into the room and mounted their attacks on him. They also shot at Hazi, forcing her to seek protection behind a pillar and leave Baugi on his own. Baugi yelped when shot in the hip. He fell to his knees, swinging harmlessly at his attackers. A soldier swung a sword and sliced Baugi's throat. The giant collapsed to the ground.

"No!" Hazi yelled, breaking her cover to launch an attack, but the guards, who were no longer occupied with trying to suppress a giant, were able to direct their attention toward her and send a volley of bullets her way. She shielded herself behind another pillar. A platoon of redcoats ran to flank our positions, firing at us to blind us of their whereabouts. Bullets ricocheted off the pillars.

A soldier leaped into the open and ran toward me with a sword raised. My hand trembled as I discharged my weapon. My shot was good, knocking him down, and he wailed in pain. One of his companions tried to pull him to safety, but quickly abandoned his effort when I fired my pistol at him. I shot at them until the bullets ran dry. Hearing the click of an empty gun chamber, one of the redcoats stepped out into the open and aimed his pistol at me. Hoping for a miracle, I aimed my pistol at him, expecting only a click but praying for gunfire. I pulled the trigger, and the man's head snapped back. The pillar behind him was spattered with blood, brains, and bone.

I spun around to see a woman in a blue military uniform holding a gun with smoke billowing out of the barrel. She immediately barked orders, pointing her finger, directing an attack on the redcoats. It was Livia, and she brought her own army. Unlike the red uniforms with gold braids worn by the emperor's army, the new soldiers wore light-blue uniforms with silver braids. Andros, Sargin, and Abydemus fired at the red outfits until the blue uniforms could rush to our aid and provide suppressing fire.

Hazi attacked the redcoats from the opposite direction, and the blue-coated soldiers joined in her attack. Hazi replenished her arrows by pulling them out of her dead victims.

Guns began to run dry of bullets, so the redcoats charged with their swords. The bluecoats, with swords of their own, held them off. Hazi punished the redcoats with deadly blows from her spear. Splattering of blood, screams of pain, and severed body parts filled the throne room.

The bluecoats defeated their enemy with their overwhelming numbers, and within minutes, the redcoats all lay dead on the ground, flooding the area with their blood. The racket of gunfire and the clashing of swords ceased.

Hazi ran to Baugi's aid, trying to stop the bleeding from his neck, but it was too late. The giant's body was sprawled on the ground in a pool of blood. Tears streamed down the scar on her cheekbone.

"Are you okay?" Livia asked me. Her emotions of sincerity were welcoming to me. Unlike Magnus, she was like an open book. Her most prominent feeling that I picked up on was that of anger towards her brother.

"What happened?" I asked.

Livia stepped beside the giant and put a gentle hand on Hazi.

"Me taking action," she said. "I've been putting together an army to overthrow my brother. I figured now was the time." Livia turned to her captain, a hulking man with curly brown hair. "Take care of the giant's body, then go after the emperor and Cato."

"What about you?" the captain asked.

"I will need a small detachment to help me retrieve something. Once I have what I'm looking for, I will rejoin you."

The man bowed, then hauled Baugi's body away with antigravity devices. Hazi watched in silence.

Livia then returned her attention to me, tying her hair into a bun. "I've made my choice."

I turned to Livia. "What choice?" I asked.

"Whether or not to give you the scroll," she said. "I know where it is."

CHAPTER 37
MIDMORNING

We followed Livia down a corridor, trying unsuccessfully to keep our footsteps quiet.

"What's the deal between you and your brother?" I whispered to Livia.

"My brother killed our father to take the throne," she said.

"Why am I not surprised?" I asked sarcastically. "What happened?"

"My father believed in peace. He tried to push legislation that would unite this planet, but some powerful people in Midlatica were vehemently against it, including my brother. In one night, he killed several legislators who supported unification, including my father." She stopped and looked at me. "He only kept me around for my pretty face," she said with a mocking smile.

"He'll probably regret that when he finds out what you just did," I noted, resuming our trek down the corridor.

"He probably already knows. I've spent the last half century building an army of loyalists, committed to restoring the old ways," she said. "Magnus engaged in genocide both down here and on the surface, which is bad enough, but when I found out that he sent some of our ships to help the reptilians—"

"Wait! What?" I asked. "Are those ships black and rectangular?"

"Oh yes. Those are ours," she said.

"Hold on!" I stopped, grabbing her shoulder, thinking there may be a connection between the rectangular black ships and the *Gideon*. "Have you ever heard of Captain Elton Blake?" I asked, recalling the message left in the ship that Eudoxus showed me.

Livia dropped her jaw. "Blake? You've seen him?" she asked, squeezing my forearm.

"I saw a message he left on the ship we came in on," I answered. "He said his mission was successful. That he found and hid something."

"Anything else?" she asked, unable to hide her smile.

"Just a sign-off," I answered, wondering if I missed something.

"Perhaps the legends are true," Livia whispered, motioning us to keep walking.

"I'm surprised you didn't board our ship since it is yours, then," I said, eyeing ahead to ensure we were still alone.

"No, no, no," she corrected, voice echoing in the hallway. "Your ship is a Zuren ship. The Ganteep people are offshoots of the Zuren. We found and reverse engineered several Zuren ships from the First Age. However, despite our best efforts, the Zuren technology is beyond us. Your ship is an original, and there is no way we could enter that ship unless invited. The ship has a mind of its own."

"He knows that then," I said. "Magnus knows we are a threat."

"That's right," she answered. "I'm just glad you didn't say anything about Captain Blake, or your ship would have been destroyed on the spot."

"You speak like Blake is still here," I said.

"More like, still relevant," she said. "Someone is meddling from the shadows."

"Not your brother then?" I confirmed.

She shook her head. "I doubt it."

Abydemus, who kept up with us by maintaining a full trot, frowned at the conversation. "I know this is fascinating, but can we get the scroll so we can save my uncle?" he urged, heaving between each sentence.

"Uncle?" she asked.

"He's Gaylin's nephew," I answered.

"I see," she said. "My brother has your uncle, and I'm sure they are heading to the portal. After we get the scroll, we'll head that way."

"I wonder why nobody has tried to stop us yet?" I asked out loud.

Everyone froze in place with the question, listening for any sounds of life other than our own.

Livia whispered a response. "Perhaps they don't know we're here," she suggested.

"Unlikely," Hazi said. "They probably need you to lead them to the scroll. It's a safe bet that we're being followed."

We resumed our journey, where we reached a metal door with pictorial engravings of animals on it. Livia pressed down on a lever. "Let me be clear on something," she said with a softened face. "Magnus wasn't always this way. There was a time when he was loving, respectful, and quite humble." Livia released the lever, opening the door.

A vast warehouse lay before us. Crates were stacked on top of each other in long rows. We followed Livia as she navigated her way through a maze of aisles. She stopped at a crate and instructed the guards to keep a lookout. Meanwhile, she pulled out a blade and, with our help, began to open the crate. The wood cracked, and the screech of tight-fitting nails pulling loose filled our ears. The lid broke open, and the soldiers tossed it. Inside the crate, Livia lifted out a silver-plated box. She opened it to reveal a silver rod about two feet long with golden caps on each end.

There was engraved writing on the rod that I hadn't seen before but I could understand. "The legend of Kantara," I read out loud. It felt as though I was not translating the words but rather reading it through the mind of the person who wrote them.

"You can understand this writing?" Livia asked, raising her eyebrows with interest and pointing to the engravings.

I nodded, still examining the rod.

"Fascinating," Livia said. "You are the first person I've known who can translate that writing."

I ignored her comment. "Where's the paper?" I asked, "This is just a rod."

"If there was a parchment attached, it was removed before it came into our possession. Personally, I assumed the rod itself was the scroll."

"Why would you think that?" I asked.

"Watch this," she said, and twisted a cap. A digital screen appeared above the rod, displaying lines, diagrams, and writing. She handed me the scroll.

"What does it say?" I asked. The electronic words on the screens weren't translating for me.

"Don't know," she confessed. "I was hoping you could tell us."

"How old is it?" I asked.

"Impossible to determine," she said. "The scroll is time locked."

"We know," Sargin said. "How do you unlock it?"

"I guess the answer is in the engravings you just translated," she speculated.

"I'd thought this thing would be under lock, key, and a massive amount of security," I murmured.

Livia chuckled. "It's impossible to find anything in all these crates here unless you know exactly where it is. My mother forced me to remember the location of several valuables, this scroll being one of them."

I touched the digital scroll carefully. The lines began to change, forming into curves and intersecting each other. A blue dot appeared, blinking at the bottom of one of the lines. Another dot appeared, but this one was yellow, and it was blinking where several lines intersected.

"What is it trying to say?" I asked softly to myself.

Abydemus stepped forward. "Looks like intersecting timelines," he observed.

"How can you possibly know that?" I asked.

"I don't," he answered. "I'm just saying what it looks like to me."

I returned my attention to the display, and suddenly, the image made sense, as if the scroll was communicating with me. "I don't know how I know this, but you're right," I admitted. "I'm having a hard time translating these symbols though."

"I've seen that symbol before," Abydemus said, pointing to an image near the blue dot. "It was on the *Gideon*."

"If that is the case, then I'm guessing the blue dot is this scroll and the yellow dot is the location of the second scroll." The answer revealed itself in my mind as if a light bulb were turned on. "It's a map!"

A movement in the corner of my eye caught my attention. I pulled out my pistol. Suddenly, several redcoats stepped out into the aisle and ran toward us.

"They're here," I yelled, then fired my gun at them. They shot back.

A bluecoat pulled me out of the aisle. "Piece of advice," he said. "Shoot first, then talk."

The bluecoats engaged with the enemy, using the crates for their defense.

"I think that will be enough," a man said from behind. We turned around to see Cato with several squads of redcoats pointing their guns at us.

We dropped our weapons in surrender. Cato walked up to me and forced the scroll from my hand with surprising strength. "Thank you for all that wonderful insight you just provided us," he said, tapping the scroll with his fingers. "We will be sure to make good use of this information." He gave the scroll to one of the soldiers, who promptly stuck it in the pouch of a shoulder bag.

"What are you going to do with us?" Livia asked, lip quivering.

"What I must, of course," he said, then ordered one of the soldiers to hand over a sword. Cato pulled the blade out from its scabbard, then stepped up to the bluecoats and hacked down each one. Blood splattered onto Cato's face and into his open mouth. All I could do was watch as the gruesome scene unfolded.

Livia fell to her knees, clenching her fists.

Cato knelt beside her, sheathing his sword and wiping the blood off his face. With a bloody grin, he spoke. "Oh, the emperor can't wait to deal with you, young lady."

CHAPTER 38
LATE MORNING

Cato brought us outside onto an open field. Behind us was the city, and before us was a forest filled with luminescent and rustling plants. In the middle of the field stood Magnus.

Next to the emperor, Gaylin knelt with a gag in his mouth and arms tied behind his back. He was guarded by a squad of redcoats. Berossus stood nearby.

The emperor's military brigade filtered into the field. An army of reptilians stepped out from the forest. Feroxraptors with redcoat handlers took flanking positions.

Cato presented Magnus the scroll. "I believe this belongs to you." He bowed.

Magnus grabbed the scroll and pointed it at Livia. "Treachery!"

"That's right," Cato agreed. "She is treacherous."

Magnus, hearing Cato's accusation, pushed Gaylin down with his boot, then kicked him. "My beloved sister forms an army in secret to overthrow my rightful place as emperor," he snarled. "High treason!" he yelled.

"Brother," Livia called out, tears in her eyes and reaching out, beckoning for his humanity.

"I am not your brother," Magnus screamed, foaming at the mouth. "You are no sister to me!"

Berossus stepped in. "What are your orders?" he asked the emperor.

"Take my army and hunt down anyone who has sided with Livia," he said. "Stick their heads on pikes as a warning to anyone who betrays me."

"It will be my pleasure," Berossus said and walked away.

Andros fidgeted, pressing his thumbs together.

"What's wrong," I asked him.

"That reptilian soldier in the middle," he said, nodding forward, "is my brother, Ivo."

I felt confusion among the ranks of the reptilians. Unlike the throne room where I was unable to feel anything from anyone, the reptilians were not closed. Several of them felt disdain for Magnus. I stepped forward to test an assumption. "The emperor is a tyrant!" I warned the reptilians. All the reptilians stepped back in astonishment. They understood me. The emperor clenched his teeth.

Cato leaned over to the emperor. "You must kill him," he said.

"Do it," the emperor ordered his guards.

One of the soldiers pulled out his sword and marched toward me. After watching Cato hack the bluecoats to pieces in the warehouse, the idea of the same happening to me was terrifying.

I flinched when the guard lifted his sword to strike, but then his skull splattered. A split second later came the sound of a gunshot.

I turned back but saw nothing. A battle horn sounded, then another from a different direction, and then another. Next, I heard the clogs of horses trotting out of the city onto the open field. I glanced to the left to see hundreds of horses mounted by bluecoats rushing into battle.

The horses swept across the reptilian horde, striking them down with sabers. A volley of bullets tore through the bodies of our enemy. The raucous gunfire echoed across the valley.

The emperor's guardsmen, who held us prisoner and carried our weapons, turned to fight, but Hazi struck the nearest one down with a round kick. With finesse, she pulled a sword from an enemy scabbard, cut through her bindings, and freed herself. Hastily, she sliced through the other guards like they were butter, then removed our bindings. We grabbed our weapons.

Two raptors charged, but Hazi pulled her spear and rammed it into one raptor's neck, severing the creature's jugular, and gracefully threw her ax into the head of the second attacking raptor. Both animals fell dead.

Across the field, Magnus grabbed Gaylin and led him into the forest. Cato followed him with the accompaniment of several redcoats.

"He's headed to the time portal," Livia yelled.

The reptilians, hearing Livia's warning, blocked our path and regrouped for a counterattack. Bluecoats on horseback ran through them, slicing down many, but the reptilian numbers kept multiplying as they filtered into the field from the forest.

Behind us, in the city, bluecoats engaged redcoats in street warfare. Bullets swarmed around us. We dove to the ground, firing our weapons in defense.

"We need more cover," Andros yelled. "We are helpless out here!"

A reptilian charged our position and tackled Sargin, knocking the air out of his lungs. The reptilian raised his kukri to finish Sargin, but Andros leapt up and sliced through the reptilian's torso with a sword, splitting him in half. The body slid down on either side of Sargin, covering him with blood and guts.

"Are you okay?" Andros asked, extending a friendly hand toward Sargin.

"Ew," Sargin said. "That was disgusting," then Sargin aimed his pistol over Andros's shoulder, shooting a reptilian square between the eyes.

"Nice shot," Andros said.

"I was aiming for the chest," Sargin admitted. "I can't aim worth a damn."

Andros grunted. "Then I'll say, lucky shot."

Bluecoats swarmed our position and interlocked their shields to create a protective wall for us.

"Livia," the captain yelled, "we need to get you out of here."

Livia shook her head. "We need to push forward," she corrected.

"We are losing this battle," the captain said. "Let's get you back in the city where we have a fighting chance."

"We must get that scroll," she demanded.

The captain frowned, looked at the forest, and then nodded with understanding. He waved his arm forward, and bluecoats ran into the field, firing at the reptilians. Raptors thrashed at them from the flank, ravaging those on the edge, but the soldiers pressed on.

Ivo, Andros's brother, attacked several bluecoats with his kukri. He ducked and dodged, repelling their attacks, then countered with fierce blows, killing several instantly. One of the bluecoats managed to fire a shot into Ivo's chest, sending the reptilian to the ground in a convulsive state.

Andros witnessed the event. "No!" he yelled. He sprinted to his brother in the open field.

"Get back here," Sargin yelled. Andros ignored him, so Sargin broke cover and sprinted to Andros's position to help where he could. "Why am I helping you help the enemy?" Sargin asked. Andros didn't answer.

"What are they doing?" Livia asked, watching Andros and Sargin expose themselves to enemy fire.

Livia sighed, then led the group to Sargin and Andros. Once in place, they recreated their wall of shields.

Andros cradled Ivo, who, in turn, stared into his brother's eyes with shock. Sargin grabbed a field kit from one of the soldiers and tended to the injury.

"What's he doing?" Livia asked.

"They are brothers," I answered.

Ivo widened his eyes and coughed. I couldn't help but give Ivo a reassuring smile.

"I understand," Ivo gurgled, laying a hand on his brother's shoulder.

"You're going to be okay," Andros repeated over and over. Andros looked up to Sargin, tears streaming down his face. "I must save him."

Sargin finished the dressing. "Go, save your brother," he said.

Andros lifted Ivo into his arms and turned toward our rear. He breathed in and glanced at us one last time. "Thank you, Keiji," he said, then hurried into the city, turning his back on the battle.

CHAPTER 39
NEARING MIDDAY

The battle persisted. Livia's cavalry charged through the reptilian formations, opening a path for us to the cover of trees. Feroxraptors attacked the cavalry, trying to ram them with their horns, but the oversized horses and their armed riders were able to overpower the raptors with blunt force and saber strikes.

Bluecoat foot soldiers at the far right of the field were ravaged by raptors, and the ones to the far left suffered an onslaught by encircling redcoats. Reptilians attacked the bluecoats at the front, ripping into their flesh. They screamed in agony as they were shot, slit, and bitten into.

A larger pack of raptors were freed by their handlers to finish us off. They sprinted toward our small group.

"Raptors to the right!" I yelled, firing my pistol at the one closest. The other members of our party redirected their shots accordingly. A feroxraptor leapt into the air to attack me but, instead, found itself squeezed in the large talons of a dragon. With a hard landing, Enkidu crushed the raptor, then burst fire from his mouth, setting redcoats and reptilians in flames.

Enkidu whipped around toward the raptors and roared. The raptors shrank and fell to the ground and began easing their way backward. Enkidu barked. The raptors jolted up, stiffened their bodies, barked back, and then revolted against their redcoat masters. The redcoats tried to use electrical shocks to bring their raptors back to submission, but the raptors mauled their faces and began eating them.

Enkidu turned away from us, revealing Malah sitting on the dragon's back, clinging to the scales. Malah waved, and we cheered. Then he urged Enkidu to keep pursuing the enemy.

"I'll be back," Sargin said, slapping my shoulder. He sprinted across the field to our rear, into the city.

"Where is he going?" Abydemus asked.

"I have no idea," I answered, reloading my pistol.

Hazi, fresh out of arrows, defended our position with weapons from several corpses. Abydemus used his small size to run under the streaking bullets to recover weapons and replenish our armament. He pulled one of Hazi's arrows out of a body and raised it in the air. "Woohoo!" he yelled. "I found an arrow!"

"Get your head down," Hazi screamed at Abydemus. "You're not that short!"

Abydemus collected more arrows and brought them back to her.

Enkidu took flight and sprayed fire on the enemy toward our front, but a barrage of cannon fire erupted from the city, aimed at the dragon. Enkidu flew over the forest outside the range of the cannons. Once the first volley of cannon fire was complete, Enkidu dove toward the city and attacked the cannoneers, sending many of them up in flames.

The tide of the battle turned to our favor with the arrival of Enkidu and the newfound allegiance by the feroxraptors. Redcoats and reptilians alike fled into the woods.

Livia pointed at the forest where leaves rustled from those retreating. "We need to get to the portal before my brother does," she urged.

"That portal can't power up very quickly, so we have a little time," the captain said.

"No, we don't," Livia argued. "We have to go now!"

The captain lifted a set of binoculars. "That forest is swarming with the enemy," he said. "We'll never make it."

"Get down!" Hazi yelled. The ground shook, and the heat of an explosion at our rear sent a platoon of bluecoats flailing.

I grabbed the binoculars in time to see a rectangular black ship flying over the forest. It was the same kind of ship that destroyed Ganteep Outpost One.

The ship shot lightning toward Enkidu. A bolt missed the dragon, but it was close enough to send Enkidu hurtling to the ground, knocking Malah off his back.

I raced to Malah's aid. His face was blood-soaked from a wound on his forehead, and his eyes were wide in shock. "That will knock the breath out of you," Malah coughed.

The ship maintained a constant pressure on us, forcing us into the forest. The bottom of the craft emitted blue lights onto the surface of the ground, where a fresh regiment of redcoats appeared. They began firing at us even before their transport beam subsided.

"We can't keep this up!" the bluecoat captain yelled. Then a bullet struck him in the neck, sending him to the ground.

The ship above kept firing, and I scurried behind a nearby tree trunk, wrapping my head with my arms and squeezing my eyes shut to prevent dirt and debris from entering them.

Suddenly, the explosions around us stopped, and everything went silent.

The silence was broken when the ship above was rocked by an onslaught of firepower, covering it with explosions. Something was assaulting it from beyond the city.

"Who's attacking?" Livia asked. In response, the assailant revealed itself, flying over the city and firing guns and cannons mercilessly. It was the *Gideon*.

"Sargin!" I yelled. "It's Sargin! He went back and got the ship."

"That thing has weapons?" Malah laughed. "I should have guessed!"

Bluecoats cheered. Though larger, the enemy vessel was at a disadvantage to Sargin's more powerful and maneuverable ship.

Abydemus pointed upward. "They're no match for him," he touted.

Abydemus spoke too soon. Sargin's ship shook with a direct hit from cannon fire from within the city, sending it into a spin. Sargin regained control, but the *Gideon* was leaving a trail of smoke behind it.

Enkidu attacked the cannon positions while the *Gideon* maintained its attack at the enemy vessel. Within seconds, it erupted from within, proving inferior to Sargin's ship. It descended into the forest, engulfed by explosions.

Sargin then attacked the troops below but was caught off guard by a swarm of missiles. The *Gideon* was struck, and it crashed into the woodlands, igniting the trees with raging yellow flames.

"Oh no," I said, standing up, stumbling toward the crash site.

"Stay focused," Livia advised me, then pointed into the forest. "We need to get to the portal."

I turned to look at our destination, but the outlook appeared dismal. The entire pathway was blocked by debris.

"How do we get through all of that?" I asked with frustration.

Abydemus turned to Malah. "Maybe Enkidu can clear a path," he suggested, raising an eyebrow.

"How do we get him to do that?" Livia asked.

Before I could suggest an answer, Enkidu hopped into view, flexing his wings and then belting out a flame that sent debris and trees flying. The heat from the flames was excruciating at first, but soon cooled down. Before us lay a clear path to the portal station that was only about a hundred yards away.

Enkidu breathed in deeply, then let the air out of his lungs. He rested beside me. I felt his breath on my face. I had always thought that a fire-breathing dragon would smell of smoke, but I smelled none. There was, however, a scent of methane. Enkidu rolled his head, then shifted it down.

I heard a voice. *Keiji.*

I turned to Malah to see if he was the one who called out my name, but it wasn't him. Nor was it the doctor. It was another telepathic voice.

Keiji, it repeated, but the sound was only in my thoughts.

I whipped myself around to see Enkidu staring at me. "Enkidu?" I asked.

He nodded.

"I can hear your thoughts," I said out of fascination.

And I can hear you, Enkidu said telepathically. *Since the first time I met you in the Ganteep forest, I could hear your thoughts.*

"What does this mean?" I asked, not sure how to take in the idea that I was speaking to a dragon.

There is no time to explain, but let's just say that I've used my mind to protect you from those who mean you harm, such as Magnus.

"That was you?" I asked rhetorically. "Why tell me this?"

That's what the doctor wanted, so tell him you succeeded. His experiment worked, Enkidu said.

"Yes!" the doctor screamed in my head. Evidently, Enkidu heard the doctor's excitement.

You don't have much time, Enkidu warned. *You need to go now. I will cover you.*

I held out my hand, and the dragon lowered his head. I caressed his jaw. "Thank you, my friend," I said, and Enkidu rendered a soft, short dragon purr.

Malah gently nudged my shoulder, pride gleaming from his face. He then climbed onto the dragon for one last defense, and Enkidu rose to a towering height, flexing his wings to take on another flight.

Go, Enkidu said. *Now!*

Chapter 40
MIDDAY

Enkidu created a diversion by attacking at full force, using his wings to sweep, talons to crush, and fire to burn. The redcoats focused their attention on the dragon and his accompanying rider, forgetting about us completely.

We reloaded our weapons, then ran down the firebreak that Enkidu had created toward the large fenced-in building with a towering steeple. The ground was still hot from the dragon fire. The grotesque smell of singed flesh flooded the air. We hopped over roots overlying the ground and avoided the occasional sinkhole. Hazi, agile in her footing and strong in her arms, helped Abydemus overcome the obstacles.

We approached the perimeter fence and were confronted by two guards, but Hazi threw her spear and impaled one through the chest. A bluecoat shot the other. Hazi retrieved her spear.

The fence gate was unlocked, so we entered without resistance. We sprinted across the inner yard to the tower and approached a door with a panel. Livia punched in a code, and the door slid open, revealing two more guards blocking a long hallway. They raised their weapons, but our accompanying bluecoats fired on them first, killing them.

Livia led us down the hallway and turned a corner, running into a wall of five redcoats. They fired, striking Hazi in the leg, Abydemus in the arm, and a bluecoat in the hip, and killed two other bluecoats. The bluecoats behind us shot at the redcoats, killing four of them. The final redcoat ran away down the hall, but Hazi dropped him with a throw of her ax, paralyzing him from the neck down.

Hazi limped to the moaning redcoat, pressed her foot into the man's neck to leverage herself, and then pulled the ax from his back. He bellowed in pain, but the noise was cut off as Hazi hacked through his head, splitting it, then returned the ax to her belt.

"How much farther?" Hazi asked, grasping her spear with both hands.

"Not much," Livia said, hopping over the dead bodies and sprinting down the corridors. The bluecoat shot in the hip was left behind.

Hazi inspected the wound on her leg and assessed it to be superficial. She took a deep breath and commenced following Livia. Abydemus grabbed his elbow below the spot where a bullet scraped his arm, hurrying to keep up. Behind him, the remaining bluecoats and I followed.

We rounded a corner to see a door at the end of the hall. When we reached it, Livia put in a code and grabbed the handle. "Are you ready?" When we nodded, she pulled open the door and was welcomed by a storm of bullets, dropping two bluecoats instantly. The rest ran in, firing their weapons at the enemy. Inside, redcoats shot back, but the unexpected rush caught them off guard, causing them to lose footing and aim. The bluecoats quickly dispatched them.

We rushed in behind the bluecoats. The room was spacious, cylindrical, and metallic, with control panels lining the walls, lights blinking on each one. Toward the rear was a glowing platform emitting a hum caused by vibrating gears and static electric poles.

Magnus was at the display. He took cover behind his remaining troops, along with three men in white lab coats. Gaylin lay on the floor, still gagged with his arms restrained. The scroll was not visible.

An unexpected fist backhanded me, splitting my lip. I looked up through bleary eyes to see my attacker, who was now running to take cover behind a workstation. It was Cato.

Anger swelled up within me. "Who the hell are you?" I screamed at Cato.

Cato laid his hand on his chest. "I'm a humble servant."

"Tell me why you are doing this!" I demanded.

"To correct a mistake. Men were meant only to be slaves," Cato said, standing up and pounding his chest, then immediately dove behind a workstation when a bluecoat fired at him. Cato laughed out loud. "We will correct the abomination known as man! This planet was never meant for you," he yelled in defiance.

Livia attempted to reason with Magnus. "Brother!" she called out. "Cato is only using you. You are just a man too in Cato's eyes! Can't you see that?"

"I am emperor," Magnus yelled, pushing the men in white lab coats to attack. They were shot by the bluecoats the instant they stepped into the open.

Magnus pulled out a double-edged blade from his sleeve and ran at us with unbridled rage. I shot at him but was thrown to the ground by some unknown force. I lifted my head to see that Magnus was also sliding across the floor, but in the opposite direction. This was the same thing that happened to Gaylin when Magnus tried to kill him. Magnus was like Gaylin. He couldn't be killed.

Cato laughed, clapping his hands. "The sister is wrong," he said with glee. "Magnus is not a man. He's a god!"

The firing stopped at the sudden revelation. Cato stepped into the open, reached down, and lifted Magnus, who inspected himself and discovered he was unharmed, to his feet. Magnus grabbed the knife from the ground.

"I am a god," Magnus grinned. "I am a god!" he repeated with a scream.

"Yes, your highness," Cato said. "Didn't I promise you great things?"

Magnus straightened his posture and walked toward me even as the bluecoats maintained their aim on the emperor. "You should bow to your god," Magnus insisted.

I looked at Gaylin, still on the floor and unable to move. "I've never been in a room with two gods before," I said, nodding to Gaylin.

"Two?" Magnus asked, stepping up and patting my face. "I see," he said, glowering down at Gaylin. With a raised eyebrow, he focused his attention on the bluecoats, who still trained their weapons on him. "You shouldn't take sides with a mortal," Magnus warned, then gave a quick glance to Livia. "Do you think that maybe she is a goddess?" he asked the bluecoats. "Why don't we see?"

"Magnus, no!" Livia begged, but Magnus shoved a knife into her abdomen so deep that only the shank remained exposed. Livia coughed up blood and fell into her brother's hands.

"Fire at him!" I ordered the bluecoats.

"I can't," one of the soldiers said. "My finger won't move."

I turned to Hazi. "Do something!" I yelled.

"I can't," she said through tight lips.

Abydemus peered up at me. "It's like I'm paralyzed," he said, trembling as he tried to wiggle his arms.

I grabbed a pistol and pointed it at Magnus, but my body froze, unable to pull the trigger.

"Now, now," Cato teased, easing his way toward us. "So much death." Cato held up a hand that was distorted in the light, as though he were projecting his will. Cato wielded a mystical power or magic.

I attempted to reason with the emperor. "What's the point in all of this? Do you think going forward in time will change anything? Even if you could, how will you get back?"

"Such a naive young boy," Cato laughed, not focusing on Livia. "Magnus isn't going anywhere. I'll take Gaylin and carry out his execution."

"Brother," Livia gasped, blood flowing out of her mouth. "This isn't you."

Magnus bowed his head to his sister, smearing blood on his face. "Then who am I?" he seethed.

"Your father's son," she said, and with her pistol she fired at Cato, then died, dropping the weapon.

Control returned to my body, and I pointed my pistol at Cato, who was clutching at his stomach. "What are you?" I asked, but the bluecoats killed him before he could answer.

Magnus shook his head, as if coming out of a trance. He tightened his hold on his sister's body. "Livia!" he screamed. "No!" The wailing of an emperor filled the room.

CHAPTER 41

Pain and remorse poured out of Magnus and permeated every fiber of my being. The loss of his sister was so intense that I felt it equaled the loss I experienced when my father died. Magnus rocked back and forth, cradling her body. "I'm so very sorry," he sobbed, running his fingers through her hair, tears streaming down his face.

"Was he under some kind of spell?" Hazi asked.

I shrugged in response. "Emperor Magnus," I called, then knelt beside him.

He looked up, revealing the soft eyes of a gentle and kind man. "I remember everything," he admitted, "and I am so sorry."

"It wasn't your fault," I said, assured by the feelings he emanated.

"Help me," he requested, lifting his sister up.

I took hold of her blood-soaked body and raised her off the emperor's lap. With his help, I gently laid her on the ground next to him, then pulled the emperor up to his feet.

On the floor, Gaylin screamed with a muffled voice through a gag, trying to attract our attention. Hazi cut him free, and then he stood, straightened his clothes, and was swooped into his nephew's embrace.

Magnus used his sleeve to wipe at the blood on his face, removing only some of it. "I will help you," Magnus said, then stumbled to a workstation and opened a drawer, revealing the scroll. Magnus handed the two-foot metallic rod to me. "Do you know what to do with this?" he asked.

"It has a map," I said. "That is about all I know. Do you know anything about this scroll that can help me?" I asked, tightening my grip on the scroll. "Anything about the legend of Kantara maybe?" The scroll grew warm at the mention of Kantara and began to glow. "Wow!"

"That's new," Magnus said, also surprised by the scroll's reaction. "Kantara, eh? My mother had mentioned Kantara before. It's a word of the gods, and it has existed since the universe sparked into being."

"What does it mean?" I asked.

"Bridge," Magnus answered. "If I remember correctly."

"Kantara," I whispered, feeling the instantaneous warmth from the scroll. I looked down in time to see the glow of the rod soften.

I took a deep breath, looking into the portal at the center of the room. The gears ceased their movement, leaving only the sound of a soft hum. The ceiling disappeared as a bright beam of light shot vertically up, opening another portal into infinity.

"Is this a time portal?" I asked. "Why did you create this?"

"I didn't," Magnus said. "This thing uses a technology that is beyond our level of comprehension."

"I don't understand," I said.

"The Council of Nine had it built," Magnus said. "You need to go."

"I don't think so," called out a voice.

Berossus and several squads of redcoats raced into the room, firing their weapons and killing two bluecoats immediately. The rest of us dove behind a computer terminal.

"Put down your arms," Magnus screamed. "That's an order!"

"They aren't going to listen to you," Berossus yelled back. "They are under my control."

"You're like Cato," Abydemus yelled, putting pieces of the puzzle together.

"No. I'm much more powerful than Cato," Berossus bragged "Sergeant Rahn," he called over to one of the redcoats. "Restrain the emperor and Gaylin. Kill the rest." Berossus grabbed the sergeant by the sleeve. "And don't let anybody through that portal."

Sergeant Rahn gave orders, and the redcoats attacked. We were desperately outnumbered. I held tightly to the scroll with one hand while firing my weapon with the other. Magnus slapped a button at the top of a workstation console.

A long roll of thunder cracked in the room, forcing everyone down, holding tightly to their ears. The light at the bottom of the portal turned to bright yellow.

Magnus grabbed me by the jacket. "The scroll will direct you," he said. "All my hopes." He gave me a gentle smile, and with surprising speed and strength for such a slender man, he threw me into the light.

***

The sun beat down on me with an orange glow. Ocean waves swept forward, covering my feet. My father lifted me up by my arms, then walked into the ocean, leaving me alone on the beach. The farther he walked, the higher the water rose, until he disappeared from my view. I watched without emotion, then heard the voice of the doctor. "Keiji."

"Keiji," the doctor repeated.

The ocean and beach dissolved, but the sun remained. "Where am I?" I asked. My tongue stuck to the roof of my mouth as I tried to speak. My eyes refused to open, like they were glued shut.

"Where you're supposed to be," the doctor reassured. "Open your eyes."

"He's waking," a voice called out.

I rubbed my eyes. A woman in a long dress and a bonnet leaned over me. "Good morning."

"Good morning," I greeted in return, trying to lift myself up, but with no success. "Where am I?" I mumbled.

"In a safe place," she reassured.

"What is that supposed to mean?" I asked, opening my mouth and touching my dried tongue.

"A safe place," she repeated. "You have some guests waiting," she said with optimism. "I'll bring them in."

I pushed myself up with my arms, holding tightly on to the frame of the bed beneath me. *I was in a bed!* The bed was made of a metal frame. It seemed like something from the mid-twentieth century. The metal frame dissolved into a wooden frame, as though I moved back in time while sitting still. It no longer felt like the twentieth century.

The door creaked open at the end of the hall, and three people, joined by the lady who was attending me, entered the room.

They stepped into the window light, revealing their faces.

"Hazi! Abydemus!" I cried, sitting up. Despite their familiarity, there was something different about them. They no longer wore their Second Age outfits, but rather the dark-blue uniforms of American naval sailors. "You made it!"

Hazi embraced my hand. She appeared a few years older with traces of gray in her hair. Despite the military uniform, she still wore braids, tucked under her hat.

"We did," Hazi said, but there wasn't any delay between the words and the movement of her mouth.

"You're speaking English," I said.

"I am," she confirmed, stepping aside to let Abydemus reach me.

"We aren't the only ones who made it," Abydemus said, grasping my hand. "Malah, Sargin, and Andros are here too!"

"But how?" I asked.

"Don't worry about that now," Hazi said. "I'd like to introduce you to someone." She stepped to the side. "This is Captain Elton Blake."

The man I saw in the *Gideon*'s holographic message entered the light.

"It's you!" I blurted, feeling a sense of déjà vu.

Blake gave a broad smile. "Welcome to the nineteenth century, young Keiji," Blake said, then lifted a two-foot metallic rod and handed it to me. "As the traveler, I believe you will be needing that."

EPILOGUE
FAR INTO THE FUTURE

Scipio leaned into his staff, watching Moti with discerning eyes. "Did he accomplish his mission?" he asked.

"Yes," Moti replied. "The traveler acquired the scroll and contacted Captain Blake, just as planned. They will soon be on their way to retrieve the second scroll."

The sentinel furrowed his brow at Moti. "Things didn't go as planned," he corrected. "That nuclear explosion by Radau? He sent a message."

"Oh, did he?" Moti said, feigning ignorance.

"You can see my concern?" Scipio asked.

"No, I do not," Moti replied, waving him off. "I have concerns of my own. Cato and Berossus. Who were they?"

"Two beings lost in time," Scipio said, pacing to the side.

Moti leaned forward. "They should not have been there," he said. "I know. I was there."

Scipio scowled at Moti. "If I didn't know better, I'd think you were accusing me of something," he said.

Moti stepped away from the sentinel. "I will update you when we have the second scroll."

***

Moti entered the control room where scientists monitored the timestream. He approached a woman sitting before a display screen and tapped her shoulder. "Where's the doctor?" he asked, not recognizing her.

She pointed to an enclosed booth. Moti thanked her and headed in the direction she pointed.

"You in there, Doctor?" Moti asked, standing outside the booth.

"Yes," the doctor said. "Keiji is sleeping, so I am just running some tests."

"I think your suspicions about Scipio may have some validity." Moti rubbed his hands together.

The doctor swiped open a curtain, then stepped out to meet him.

Moti Magnus put his hand on the shoulder of his longtime friend, Doctor Gaylin. "Scipio knows we suspect his involvement," Magnus said, "but with Blake in the picture now, we have the upper hand."

"I will make sure it stays that way," Gaylin replied. "Did Scipio question you about our diversion to Ganteep?"

"Doesn't have a clue," Moti said, "and he most certainly knows nothing about Keiji's success with Enkidu."

"Don't be so sure," Gaylin warned, then returned to the booth, swiping the curtain shut.

Moti exited the lab and stepped into a corridor that stretched endlessly down each side. It was enclosed with windows revealing that he was standing on the surface of the moon. The blue-green planet known as Earth hung in the sky.

A man appeared out of thin air, staring at Moti with searching gray eyes. It was Admiral Radau. "The message was received," he said, referring to the one sent when he exploded the *Nemesis*.

"I know," Moti said.

"Seeking an enemy who does not want to be found will be dangerous," Radau warned.

"We don't have a choice," Moti said.

Admiral Radau forced a smile, then stepped through the wall onto the moon's surface like he was a ghost.

Moti laid a hand on the windowsill, watching Radau walk into the horizon. He left footprints in the moondust, reminding Moti that he was not a ghost after all.

A dark plume suddenly erupted from an underground facility, averting Moti's attention from the admiral. Even in the vacuum of space, the plume moved above like a cloud on Earth. Moti returned his attention back to the mysterious figure, but Radau was nowhere to be seen.

"The moon holds the answer," he said to himself. "I know it!"

LIST OF ILLUSTRATIONS